'I'm not in a smiling mood, Blake. Frankly, I don't know why I came when I've nothing at all to say to you!'

The glow of his smile was reflected in his eyes, blinding Jenefer to the shadow of hurt in their depths. 'Then just sit back and enjoy your drink and let me do the talking.'

'Sweet-talking, no doubt! You were always very good at that.'

'You liked to hear it once upon a time.'

'Once upon a time is apt! When I was still young enough to believe in fairy stories! I've grown up, Blake. You don't impress me any more.'

Lynne Collins has written twenty-five Doctor Nurse Romances based on personal experience of hospital life backed by research and information from her many friends in the medical profession. She likes writing about hospital settings, with their wealth of human interest. Married with one son and now living on the Essex coast, Lynne enjoys travel, meeting people, talking, walking and gardening. She has also written several Doctor Nurse Romances under the pen-name of Lindsay Hicks.

STAR
SURGEON

BY

LYNNE COLLINS

MILLS & BOON LIMITED
ETON HOUSE   18-24 PARADISE ROAD
RICHMOND   SURREY   TW9 1SR

*First published in Great Britain 1989
by Mills & Boon Limited*

© Lynne Collins 1989

*Australian copyright 1989
Philippine copyright 1989
This edition 1989*

ISBN 0 263 76420 6

*Set in Plantin 11 on 11 pt.
03 – 8905 – 54322*

Typeset in Great Britain by JCL Graphics, Bristol

Made and Printed in Great Britain.

CHAPTER ONE

OUT OF THE CORNER of an eye, Jenefer saw a flash of a tall, broad-shouldered figure with strong, handsome profile capped by gleaming black hair. Her heart faltered and she caught her breath on a gasp of shock, spinning in the driving seat to look more closely at the man who bounded up the stone steps of the main entrance of Pagett's.

Then she pulled herself together, mocking the absurd fancy that she had glimpsed someone who had once been more than a friend. As if *he* would be *here*, in Penfold, disappearing through the doors of the local hospital!

A trick of the light, she decided, backing her brown Fiat into its reseved bay. Or the inevitable result of he recurring images that had haunted her for several days, although she had thought him long forgotten, no longer part of her dreams or her destiny.

Heaven knew why he had come to mind so vividly or so vainly after so long. The time of the year, perhaps. She had met him in the spring. A chance word, maybe. Or perhaps an old film that she had scarcely registered while switching television channels. Triggers for the subconscious, according to all the psychologists, she told herself lightly, and turned the key firmly on the private store of memories as she locked her car and headed for the plate-glass entrance doors.

However, walking across the Main Hall, she glanced round for another sight of that tall figure to confirm that it *had* only been a fancy. She crossed the wide reception area with its central desk and comfortably furnished waiting areas, its tea-bar and high-strung television screen for the benefit of patients and their relatives, its many doors and corridors leading to a number of clinics and departments and administration offices. There were plenty of people milling about, but not one resembled the man she had in mind.

With a dismissive shrug of slim shoulders, Jenefer continued towards the lifts that connected with the wards, a slender girl in her dark blue dress, small waist cinched by the wide black belt with its gleaming silver buckle, cap pinned securely amid the cluster of chestnut curls that framed a pale oval face, grave in repose so that she seemed rather older than her years but warming to near-beauty and obvious, glowing youth with her lovely smile.

That smile sparkled in response to a number of friendly greetings as she waited for the lift.

'Good morning, Sister.'

'Nice weekend, Sister?'

'Good to see you back, Sister.'

'Hallo, Sister! Did you enjoy your break?'

She had only been away for a few days, but it was nice to be missed, Jenefer thought warmly, pushing open the heavy swing doors that guarded entry to Cresswell, Women's Medical.

She paused to survey the ward with its double row of beds and array of clinical equipment and the long emergency trolleys positioned at intervals down the long room. The early greyness of the morning had given way to spring sunshine that streamed through tall windows to cast rectangular patches of gold across the beds and the polished floor.

Spring flowers were crammed into a variety of vases on each locker, together with colourful get-well cards, bowls of fruit and bottles of squash, boxes of tissues, water jugs and beakers and an assortment of personal possessions. Every morning, the lockers were cleared and polished and by the end of each day they were again crowded with a muddled array of articles.

Jenefer was very strict about hygiene, but she wasn't too fussy about tidy lockers, feeling that the patients needed to have whatever added to their comfort or peace of mind close to hand. In her view, rigid adherence to the rules was as old-fashioned as the high-crowned, frilly organza cap that was only worn by Ward Sisters at the Pagett Foundation Hospital.

But she wore that cap with pride.

Her senior staff nurse was in the office, having taken Report and delegated jobs to the juniors and then sat down to deal with some of the routine paper work. She greeted Jenefer with a relieved smile.

'Am I glad to see you back!' she declared.

'Tell me the worst,' Jenefer invited as she stowed her bag in a drawer of the filing cabinet.

'Mrs Lennox died, Mrs King haemorrhaged, Miss Hamilton had a relapse, Nurse Wilmot went sick with shingles.' Brenda ticked items off on her fingers as she recounted the traumas of the last few days. 'Dr Montague read the riot act to an agency nurse who upset a patient and she walked out in a huff. We've had four admissions and two new juniors, one hopeless and one not so bad, and Hilda's been asking for you non-stop. And that's just for starters!'

'Pretty routine by the sound of it! Never mind, I'll take over now and you can slip away and have a nervous breakdown in your coffee break,' Jenefer soothed.

'I think I'd *enjoy* a breakdown after the hassle we've had over the weekend! How was *your* weekend?'

Jenefer reached for the Report Book. 'I went to Bristol to help my sister move house. My eldest nephew has measles, the baby has bronchitis, my brother-in-law fell and fractured his wrist, the dog ran away, nobody could find the electric kettle and my sister had one of her migraines. I should have stayed at home!'

'And I thought *we* were having a bad time,' Brenda sympathised with a grin. 'But you coped, I expect. You always do.'

She was always *expected* to cope, Jenefer thought wryly. Wasn't she the sensible Gale girl, level-headed and practical, so useful in an emergency, who had naturally progressed from bandaging dolls and playmates to real patients and done so well that she had been crowned with a Sister's frilly cap as a reward?

While happy-go-lucky Jocelyn floated from crisis to crisis in lighthearted, prettily helpless fashion, rushing into marriage and motherhood straight from school, always in debt and never worrying about anything. *When in trouble send for Jenefer* was her motto—and Jenefer was always unfailingly there when needed. Coping, like a good sister.

She coped with her own problems too, locking heartache and disappointment into a secret compartment unsuspected by family or friends who thought she had found everything she wanted in nursing. And so she had, Jenefter told herself firmly, chasing away the ghost of herself at eighteen and in love, as Brenda went off to her coffee break and she took the reins of her ward back into her capable hands.

Surprised and flattered by the offer of a ward of her own, she had leaped at the chance to fulfil the dream of early training days. Used to hard work and responsibility, knowing just how to deal with doctors and surgeons who could be autocratic and demanding, liked by fellow nurses and popular with patients, she had coped with a variety of problems in the past six months. Now her ward was the most important thing in Jenefer's life.

Making a routine round of the ward, she paused beside a bed where a middle-aged woman was being tube-fed by a first-year, a new addition to Jenefer's team of nurses and still an unknown quality. Rather older than most student nurses, she had taught at a primary school before deciding that she wanted to nurse, and Jenefer wasn't sure that the girl would be an asset to Cresswell. Sick people and unruly infants had little in common, she thought dryly.

She saw signs of distress in Mrs Maitland's florid face and feeble gestures. Admitted after a stroke that had left her partially paralysed and with impaired speech and sight, she had a spirit that refused to admit defeat. Jenefer had become fond of someone she regarded as a lovely lady and a general favourite with everyone.

'Just a moment, Nurse Morley,' she said crisply, whisking bright chintz curtains about the bed. She smiled at Hilda Maitland and made a slight adjustment to the angle of the feeding tube. 'I think you'll find that's better. The feed was flowing too fast.'

'Thank you, Sister.'

Jenefer stayed to approve the girl's steady hand and the cheerful chat that was intended to take Hilda's mind off the unpleasant business of being fed by tube.

'That's much better,' she nodded, knowing the value of a little praise to leaven the seemingly endless criticism and rebuke that was the usual lot of student nurses. Sometimes it seemed a long time since her own training days, but she hadn't forgotten how it felt to be at the lowest end of the hospital hierarchy.

Checking the watch she wore pinned to the bodice of her dark blue dress, she wondered if she could safely leave the new junior to finish the feed without further supervision. There was a huge pile of paperwork sitting on her desk in the ward office.

Cresswell was a busy ward with a constant stream of admissions and doctors coming and going at all hours, day and night. Through the drawn curtains, Jenefer heard the sound of a nurse's brisk step as she hurried along the ward, the chink of a metal receiver against a trolley top, the steady bleep of a cardiac monitor, the quiet voice of Brenda Walsh as she carried out the drugs round with one of the juniors to check each dosage against the patient's chart and the persistent ring of an unanswered telephone. Familiar, everyday sounds to the Sister who had been in charge of the ward for almost six months.

Someone silenced the telephone. The steps slowed to a halt and Jenefer listened to the soothing tones of Nurse Abbott as she spoke to the seriously ill patient in the next bed. Further down the ward, the drugs trolley renewed its distinctive rumble as the staff nurse went on with the round.

Cresswell was behaving like a well-run ward that morning, she thought thankfully. There were days when she came close to wishing that she had never taken on the responsibility for an acute medical ward, however. She hoped this wasn't going to be one of them.

'Sister . . .!'

Collecting her wandering thoughts at the urgent note in the junior's voice, Jenefer realised that Hilda Maitland was uttering choked sounds and making anxious, fluttery gestures with her good hand.

Her training told her there was no real cause for alarm. Hilda was more annoyed than agitated. She moved into range of her limited vision and bent over the bed. 'What's the matter, Hilda? Don't you want any more?' Hilda shook her head so furiously that she threatened the tube that extended from her nose. Jenefer patted her shoulder reassuringly. 'All right, Nurse,' she said over her own shoulder, 'that will do. How much of the feed has she taken?'

'About two-thirds, Sister.'

Jenefer beamed approval. 'But that's splendid, Hilda,' she enthused. 'You've done really well.' She turned to Nurse Ann Morley. 'Clean the tube as you were shown in PTS and clear everything away as quickly as you can. Ask Nurse Walton to help you to get Hilda into a clean nightie and change her sheets.' She squeezed the patient's clinging hand. 'I'll come back and talk to you later, my love,' she promised with a warm smile, seeing the questions that crowded into the anxious eyes.

Jerking her hand away, Hilda dug herself violently in the chest and then pointed at Jenefer, again and again, beseeching her with anxious gaze and guttural sounds.

The junior looked alarmed, but seven years of nursing had taught Jenefer to recognise the main anxieties of patients, and particularly of stroke victims. The loss of speech was always a cruel blow, but it was alleviated to some extent in Hilda's case, for she could write with her left hand, although the frantic scrawls on innumerable scraps of notepaper were often illegible because of her mental confusion. An experienced nurse could often guess at the need or concern that tried so hard to express itself on paper or with gestures and facial contortions and those pitiful attempts at speech.

'No, I won't forget,' Jenefer assured her warmly, knowing that patients often felt they were in danger of being neglected, although seldom an hour passed without some kind of nursing care. Time dragged for the patients in their beds, but it flew for the staff and there were never enough hours in Jenefer's busy day.

With anguished appeal in the shadowed eyes and a little moan, Hilda clutched at Jenefer's hand and dragged it towards the hated tube.

She patted the flushed cheek. 'Not just yet, I'm afraid,' she said gently. 'But soon. Dr Montague is coming to see you this morning and I'll talk to him about it. He's bringing a new doctor with him,' she went on brightly in an effort to divert the suddenly dejected Hilda as she sank back on her pillows. 'Do you remember?' Hilda had been told several times but soon forgot what was said to her. 'There's nothing for you to worry about, though. You're doing very well and we're all very pleased with you.'

She left Hilda looking less anxious and trying to smile at the junior nurse as she began to disconnect the feeding apparatus. A little encouragement and hope for the future went a long way with patients who despaired at times of ever being well again. Jenefer wished it was possible to convince stroke victims in particular in the early days that their chances of a return to near normal living were much better than they or anxious relatives could visualise.

On her way to the office, Jenefer paused to

straighten a sheet, to adjust a pillow, to admire a
newly-arrived card or a family photograph. She
picked up a box of tissues for one patient, a dropped
newspaper for another. She noticed an empty water
jug and told a passing junior to bring a fresh supply.
Her warm smile made everyone feel a little better,
although she was unaware of its potency.

She spent some time with an old lady who was
seriously ill with bronchial pneumonia and
progressive heart failure, checking pulse and counting
respirations and adjusting the face mask as she noted
the level of oxygen in the tall cylinder beside the bed.
A new one would soon be needed.

Leaving Miss Hamilton, she wondered if she had
time for coffee, and a glance through Hilda's case-
notes so that she had all the relative facts at her
fingertips when Ryan Montague came to the ward
with a new registrar, who was said to have achieved
some remarkable results from surgery in stroke cases.

Too late, she realised ruefully, as the ward doors swung
back to admit two men in long white coats and she saw
the gleam of Ryan's blond head in a shaft of sunlight.

Jenefer hurried into the office to take off the frilled
organza cuffs that protected her rolled-up sleeves.
Thrusting them out of sight in a drawer, she hastily
unrolled her sleeves and fastened buttons and slipped
starched linen cuffs over the wrists. Pagett's had
retained many of its traditions while keeping pace
with new treatments and modern surgical procedures,
and Ward Sisters weren't supposed to receive visiting
doctors while wearing their 'frills'.

It was an irritating rule and Jenefer didn't always
comply with it, depending on the doctor in question.
She was so often needed to help her nurses with
routine ward work that she could have spent much of

the day whipping cuffs on and off as consultants came and went, she thought dryly. However, the new registrar was an unknown quantity who just might be stuffy enough to take umbrage if she didn't show him the respect traditionally due to a senior surgeon.

She was flipping through files in the cabinet when Ryan tapped lightly on the open office door. She turned to him with the ready smile that warmed and widened gold-flecked hazel eyes.

'Good morning, Dr Montague!' The warmth of her lilting voice betrayed her liking for the young doctor who was also a friend. 'You've come to see Mrs Maitland, of course. I have her file right here . . .' The words trailed off as Jenefer looked beyond Ryan to his tall colleague and her smile froze.

Her heart jolted to a halt, then leapt wildly in her breast. That tall figure with the unmistakable crop of black curls and those splendid shoulders and that purposeful stride had not been a figment of her imagination, after all! But what on earth was Blake doing *here*? At Pagett's!

Ryan didn't seem to notice the suddenly heightened atmosphere as surgeon and Ward Sister appraised each other warily.

'Mr Armstrong from the NSU has come along to have a look at our Hilda,' he announced lightly. 'He's had a lot of experience of such cases and may be able to do something for her.' He glanced from one to the other, becoming sensitive to the hint of tension in the room. 'I don't know if you two know each other . . .?'

'No!' Jenefer blurted the instinctive, unwise denial on an insane impulse, and was relieved that Blake's only response was to look at her with a lift to a slanting black brow. The usually unruffled Ward Sister had temporarily lost her poise, and colour crept into her face as she hastily glanced away.

'Oh, in that case—Blake Armstrong . . . Sister Jenefer Gale,' Ryan obliged.

Jenefer smiled perfunctorily at the man she had once expected to marry. 'Mr Armstrong,' she said in brisk acknowledgement, her tone as crisp and as cool as if she had never seen him before in her life. She had certainly never wanted to see him again, she thought bitterly, as old feelings and long-suppressed memories stirred and surged.

Blake nodded. 'Sister.'

His deep-set dark eyes showed none of the shock and surprise that she felt, and Jenefer suspected that he had been better prepared than herself for this encounter. If only she had listened when Ryan spoke so enthusiastically about the new senior registrar from the Neuro-surgical Unit! But she had been busy, her mind on so many other things, and Armstrong was a very ordinary surname. It certainly hadn't occurred to her to link it with a man she had known in her Hartlake days.

Ryan hadn't mentioned his first name—and who would suppose that a man with a high degree of ambition and an almost guaranteed future at a famous London hospital would take a job at a small provincial hospital like Pagett's? As she remembered it, Blake had set his sights on a consultancy and a private practice with rooms in Harley Street!

Jenefer realised that one mystery at least was solved. Her subconscious must have registered the name, and all its implications, and begun to plague her with those persistent reminders of the past. She had been too involved with Jocelyn's problems to have the time or the inclination to trace the source of those haunting and unwelcome memories to a casual mention of the newcomer to the NSU, however.

Now, her chin tilted at the hint of mockery in his tone and his slight smile.

Blake held out a peremptory hand. 'May I see the notes, Sister?'

'Certainly.' Jenefer passed the file with a bright, professional smile, carefully not encountering his eyes. Or his touch.

'How's Hilda?' Ryan leaned against a filing cabinet, arms folded across his chest. Fair-haired and blue-eyed, he was good-looking and very personable. But, having known him for much of his life, Jenefer took his physical attractions and winning charm for granted.

'She hasn't had a very good night, I'm afraid. She doesn't like the nasal tube at all, as you know. The night staff had to tie her good hand to the bed-rail after twice getting the duty houseman out of bed to put it back. She doesn't like the bed-rail either. It offends her dignity. On top of everything else, she doesn't like the idea of being examined by yet another doctor,' Jenefer finished dryly.

'I can't say I blame her—she's seen too many of us already. But I'm sure that Blake can help in her case. He's an expert in his field and I feel we're particularly fortunate to have someone with his amount of experience working at Pagett's.'

Jenefer smiled frostily. Intent on reading the case-history, Blake Armstrong didn't glance up at the admiring mention of his skills. He was too used to accolades, she thought coldly, recalling the young surgeon at Hartlake who seemed to have everything going for him.

'How about her speech? Any improvement, Sister?'

'Not yet. That upsets her very much too. But she manages to make herself understood one way or another, Doctor. She's a very forceful lady.' Her smile softened the slightly formal tone. They weren't usually so stiff with each other in the comparative privacy of the ward office.

She wondered if they both felt inhibited by Blake. As Ryan's attention was drawn to the notes by a quiet word from the surgeon, she also wondered if he was a little overawed by the reputation and the dominant personality of the darkly handsome man who was just as Jenefer remembered, with the addition of a few silver streaks among the deep waves and crisp curls of his jet-black hair.

She studied the ward through the panoramic window while the two men discussed diagnosis and prognosis and surgical possibilities. Curtains were still drawn about Hilda's bed, she observed, automatically noting details even as memories scuttled through her mind like panic-stricken mice.

Her heart thudded and she felt slightly sick. It was the shock of seeing Blake again after so long, of course. Five years. Or was it six? She had put him out of her mind and her life so successfully that she wasn't sure. Yet, once upon a time, it would have seemed impossible to forget even the smallest detail concerning their affair.

Maturity suited him. But he had always been dangerously attractive, tall and lean-hipped and broad-shouldered with chiselled good looks and dancing dark eyes. Plus a smile to capture a girl's heart and sweep her into loving.

Star surgeon at Hartlake, handsome and charismatic, it was no wonder that so many of her fellow nurses had sighed over him and envied Jenefer when she was briefly the number one girl in Blake Armstrong's life.

But those days were long gone.

CHAPTER TWO

'WELL, you're the expert. But in my humble opinion, there won't be any real improvement in her condition without surgical intervention,' Ryan was insisting as Jenefer wrenched her thoughts back to the present.

'I've studied the results of the scan and I agree with you that the aneurism might well be tied off or excised at an acceptable degree of risk. But I'm not convinced that it's the real culprit in this case,' Blake said firmly.

'So what do you suggest?'

Blake tapped the notes in his hand. 'According to the record, Mrs Maitland has a history of minor cerebral spasms since childhood, and that indicates a congenital condition, surely. In my view, the aneurism itself is relatively harmless. But she was admitted last year after a coronary and tests showed considerable narrowing of the aortic artery. I'm inclined to suspect a thrombosis that isn't showing up on the scan . . .'

Jenefer listened to Blake's deep, determined voice with mixed feelings, recalling how warmly caressing it had sounded when he asked her to marry him—and how harsh and cold it had been when he said things she could never forgive during that last, bitter quarrel.

Deeply hurt, she had wrenched his ring from her finger and hurled it at him. 'You can go to hell, Blake Armstrong—and take this with you!' she had stormed, and she had never forgotten the smile of something very like satisfaction in his dark eyes as Blake pocketed the beautiful emerald and walked away.

Having waited in vain for an apology or an assurance that he still loved and wanted her, Jenefer had been forced to conclude that he had changed his mind about marrying her. Certainly he had seemed very reluctant to commit himself completely or to forgo his amorous pursuit of other women!

If she couldn't trust him then she certainly didn't want to marry him, Jenefer had sensibly decided. And if she wasn't going to marry him then she didn't want to continue her nursing career at a hospital where they were both so well known. Within weeks, she had transferred to Pagett's, her home town hospital, to finish her training.

Now, her heart quieting after the initial shock, she knew that she had no regrets. Nursing had always been her first love, before and after Blake, and few girls of her age could boast a Sister's coveted cap. Not at Pagett's, anyway, where she was the youngest Ward Sister to be appointed in all its long history. She was very proud of that fact.

Marriage to Blake would have been a disaster. He was the kind who couldn't stay faithful to any woman for long—and Jenefer doubted that time had changed him one scrap as as Ann Morley paused at the office door and Blake turned to look her over with unmistakable interest.

'Yes, Nurse?' Jenefer frowned at the first-year, supposing it was inevitable that the girl's gaze should be riveted on Blake as he lounged against the desk, hands plunged into the pockets of his white coat, dark head inclined to listen to Ryan but the glow of a smile in the dark eyes that rested on the junior nurse.

'I've settled Mrs Maitland, Sister.'

It was an unnecessary report and Jenefer suspected that Ann Morley had seized an opportunity for a closer look at an attractive surgeon. 'Very well. You've twenty minutes before you go to Lecture, I think. You can tidy the linen cupboard, Nurse.'

'Yes, Sister. Thank you, Sister.' Obviously convinced that she had been despatched to the furthest corner of the ward by a suspicious senior, the first-year dared Jenefer's disapproval and ruined the effect of demure obedience by lingering to bestow a particularly fetching smile on the new registrar.

'Off you go, then, Nurse. Don't waste time!' snapped Jenefer, deciding to keep a vigilant eye on the girl whose trim figure and attractively warm personality made her a likely target for Blake's amorous attentions. While *she* was in charge of Cresswell, she would see to it that he had no opportunity to flirt with Ann Morley or any other nurse!

They could all do exactly as they pleased off duty, of course. Her responsibility for the juniors didn't extend to their private lives, thank goodness!

She turned from frowning after the departing first-year to meet Blake's dark eyes, and stiffened at the glint of sardonic amusement in their depths. Had she sounded so crisply professional, so briskly authoritative, so much like the martinets who ran the wards at Hartlake? She had once vowed that she would never be so fierce or so feared if she ever attained a ward of her own, but in those days she had not known the demands and the difficulties of the job.

Once, Blake had said bluntly that she was unsuited to the role of Ward Sister. She was too anxious to be liked and could never be strict enough with juniors or firm enough with patients, he had said in sweeping dismissal of her ambition. She became too involved with patients and their problems, and that would affect her judgement as well as her authority. She had too much heart to make a really good nurse.

Fuming, Jenefer had determined to prove him wrong. Now she admitted that everything he claimed about her had been true—*then*. Now she could handle the most rebellious nurse or bumptious houseman or recalcitrant patient with ease, and she had acquired the necessary degree of detachment for the job of Ward Sister. And she had almost forgotten that she had a heart. On or off duty . . .

Ryan closed the folder with a smile for the patiently waiting Jenefer. 'I do apologise, Sister! We seem to have taken over your office.' He turned to his colleague. 'We obviously can't decide on any course of action until you've seen the patient. So I suggest that we adjourn to the ward.'

'Certainly. But you'll need a few moments with Mrs Maitland to prepare her for my examination and I'd like to have another look at the X-rays. Go ahead, Montague. Sister and I will be along shortly.'

Ryan looked a little doubtful, but he nodded and left the office. Jenefer watched through the window as he made his way down the ward to Hilda's bed, her restless fingers marshalling stock requisition forms into a neat pile on the desk as she wondered if Blake had engineered an opportunity for a private word and what they could possibly have to say to each other after so long.

He didn't speak. He didn't even look at her as he stood before the display stand, studying illuminated X-ray plates as though he was wholly intent on familiarising himself with their information.

Jenefer had no desire to speak to him either. But they couldn't continue to pretend that they were total strangers to each other. People would only wonder and speculate all the more when it leaked out that they had known each other very well at Hartlake, as it inevitably would. She knew the efficiency of the hospital bush telegraph too well to doubt that their one-time engagement would shortly be the talk of Pagett's.

'You look much the same,' she said crisply, so coolly that it couldn't possibly be mistaken for admiration or approval. 'Every inch the successful surgeon.'

Blake turned, a mocking arch to a dark brow. 'Decided to admit that we do know each other, Sister? Very sensible!'

She felt as uncomfortable as he no doubt intended. 'You were a surprise,' she said in weak defence of that impulsive denial.

'Not a pleasant one, apparently.' Blake's smile concealed his own surprise that she had been so obviously unprepared. New staff were usually avidly discussed in any hospital and he had fully expected Jenefer to be forewarned of his arrival at Pagett's.

Jenefer shrugged. 'You were the last person I expected to walk into my ward. I imagined you to be making a name for yourself in Harley Steet.' Her tone was barbed, for she had associated his sudden wish to be free with his ambition and smarted at the implication that she was thought to be unsuited to the eventual role of consultant's wife, after all. She was sure that she had been found wanting in some way, and the dent to her pride had persisted long after the hurt to her heart had healed.

'If the thought of me ever crossed your mind.'

'I haven't cherished any fond memories of you, if that's what you mean,' she said tartly. 'But your name crops up now and again. Various friends seem to think that I'm still interested in anything that concerns you.'

He smiled. 'Friends can be so insensitive,' he drawled.

Jenefer shrivelled him with a glance. 'The last I heard was that Sir Jacob had finally decided to retire and you were in line for the consultancy.'

'I had the right qualifications and the old man's backing, and the post was mine if I'd wanted it.' Blake shrugged. 'In the circumstances, I decided not to apply.' He felt there was no need to enlarge. No doubt those self-same friends had kept her well informed of recent events.

'I daresay you had your reasons.' Jenefer spoke as if she wasn't very interested in any of them. But she was puzzled. For it wasn't like the Blake she had known to throw away a golden opportunity to achieve a long-held ambition.

She was so obviously indifferent that Blake felt chilled. 'I wanted a change,' he told her with seeming carelessness. 'Your NSU needed someone with my experience—and Penfold has an excellent golf course and is near enough to the coast for me to get in some sailing. So here I am.'

It was so bland that she immediately felt there had to be more to his rejection of a prestigious and profitable post than he was saying. Perhaps his departure from Hartlake had coincided with the threat of a damaging scandal. He was a sensual man and maybe an unwise affair with a patient or a colleague's wife had cost him the consultancy.

'And no doubt you knew that our NSU is one of the best in the country,' she suggested dryly.

'Actually, I'd heard that some of the prettiest girls in the country are Pagett's nurses. That was the real attraction.' His lazy smile brimmed with charm.

Jenefer looked at him coldly. 'You haven't changed.'

'Probably not. Whereas I hardly recognised you for all that starch. You must have worked very hard for that cap. But that doesn't surprise me, of course—I remember you as a very determined girl.'

'Pigheaded was the expression, as I recall,' she said crisply, feeling that something in his tone put her in the wrong. But what could be wrong with wanting to do well and being proud of her success? And how mean of Blake to sneer at an achievement that had substituted for the happiness she had once hoped to find with him!

Blake arched an eyebrow. 'I don't remember being that rude to you, Jenefer. I might have said stubborn,' he conceded, smiling.

'You said a lot worse than that.' Inexplicably, she was swept by a wave of renewed hurt as she thought of their last quarrel and its outcome. It was odd that she should remember so vividly her outrage and his coolness, his utter lack of excuse or explanation. She had believed then, and still did, that he had deliberately provoked her into breaking their engagement.

'I expect we both did.' Blake looked down at the slender, grave-faced girl in her dark blue dress and distinctive cap, and much more than memory stirred as he met the sparkling hazel eyes with their sweep of long, gold-tipped lashes. He was filled with a familiar regret and a renewed desire as well as a strengthening of the resolve to make another bid for his happiness that had brought him to this part of the world. 'But it wasn't all hard words and hurt feelings, Jenefer,' he reminded her lightly. 'We had some good times too, as

I recall.'

Alarm bells sounded as she encountered the melting warmth of dark eyes set deep in the lean, handsome face.

'It's a long time ago and we were two very different people,' she countered briskly, her tone and the light in her eyes warning him not to try to build on a coincidence that had brought him back into her life. She had no intention of being hurt a second time by Blake Armstrong!

Blake switched off the back-light of the display stand and turned towards the door. 'Very true—and this isn't the time or the place to discuss all the changes. Lead the way, Sister. We mustn't keep my prospective patient waiting any longer.'

The ward had never seemed so long or so unusually still as Jenefer walked at the surgeon's side between the row of beds, fluted cap just level with his broad shoulder, the rustle of her skirts vying with the squeak of her rubber soles on the polished floor. Head high, she held on firmly to her role as Sister Cresswell while wishing with all her heart that Blake hadn't turned up at Pagett's to remind her of days when she had been a very foolish first-year.

It *could* only be coincidence, surely? Unless mutual friends had kept him informed of *her* movements too! But if he had known that she was a Ward Sister at Pagett's it was much more likely that he would have taken good care to maintain the miles between them, she thought dryly, remembering the bitter parting. There must have been a dozen women in his life since herself, and he had tired of her too quickly to have cherished any lingering sentiment about her or their shortlived romance.

Blake sat on the side of Hilda's bed to talk to her

about the suggested surgery after a careful examination and a brief conference with his colleague. He was totally honest about the degree of risk, but he was careful to allay anxiety, and by the time he got to his feet with a reassuring pat of her hand and a flash of his engaging smile, Hilda had succumbed completely to his charm and acquired a childlike faith in his ability to make her well, Jenefer observed.

She paused to straighten sheets and adjust pillows. 'There, that wasn't too bad, was it?' she soothed. Hilda struggled with pencil and paper to produce an almost unreadable squiggle that she thrust at Jenefer, anxiously waiting for her to decipher the scrawl. 'Yes,' she agreed, giving Hilda a quick, affectionate hug, 'he *is* nice.'

She had never denied that Blake was nice, Jenefer thought wryly as she hurried in the wake of the two men. It was only a small part of the charm that made him such a danger to her sex.

Ryan was a familiar figure on Cresswell and scarcely a head turned to look at him as he strolled between the double row of beds in his white coat, stethoscope dangling from a pocket, talking earnestly to his companion. But Blake's impressive height and dark good looks roused considerable interest, and less seriously ill patients raised heads from pillows or sat straighter in chairs while nurses who ought to be busy elsewhere had suddenly found jobs on the ward that demanded their immediate attention.

Blake was a remarkably handsome man, Jenefer admitted fairly. She was possibly the only nurse at Pagett's with a built-in immunity to his very physical attractions, and even she couldn't help a reluctant stir of admiration. A hangover from the days when she had gone weak at the knees with longing for a mere glimpse of the good-looking young surgeon whose smile had quickened so many hearts at Hartlake, she told herself wryly. But she was no longer the impressionable eighteen-year-old who had made a fool of herself over a star surgeon.

She waited for doctor and surgeon to reach agreement, surprised that Blake seemed to be arguing against operating on Hilda. Doctors didn't always agree on diagnosis or treatment, of course. But in her experience few surgeons were reluctant to use the skill acquired through long years of training and experience.

Blake insisted on more tests before he could make a final decision, but a tentative day for the suggested surgery was pencilled into his busy schedule. Then he went away with white coat flying and dark head towering above everyone else as he strode along the corridor.

Ryan frowned at the surgeon's broad back. 'Well, what do you think of him, Jenefer? Knows how to sell himself, doesn't he? I suppose he acquired his bedside manner at Hartlake along with his surgery.'

It was the obvious moment for Jenefer to admit that she had met Blake Armstrong during her spell of training at Hartlake. But the edge to the young doctor's tone told her that he had taken a rare dislike to his new colleague, and she knew that Ryan would take up the cudgels on her behalf if he learned that Blake had caused her heartache in the past. She didn't owe him anything, but she didn't want to make things difficult for Blake in his first weeks at Pagett's.

'Hilda took to him, didn't she?' she said evasively. 'He made her laugh and she seems to trust him. It was wonderful to see her in such optimistic mood.'

'Ten minutes of smooth talking and she's convinced

that surgery can cure her and he's the man to do it. He was convincing, in view of the fact that he obviously doesn't share my conviction of what he'll find if he does operate.' Ryan glanced at his watch. 'I'm overdue in Outpatients. Make an appointment for me to talk to Mr Maitland some time today, will you, Jenefer?'

As he left, bristling, Jenefer wondered if he had sensed an implied disapproval of his readiness to resort to surgery in Blake's attitude. Certainly she felt that the insistence on more tests was a delaying tactic and she wondered if Blake felt that surgery would merely raise false hopes and do little to help in Hilda's case. But he hadn't said so, and it wasn't like the Blake she had known to be diffident. In fact, he had always been sure of himself to the point of arrogance, unafraid to take chances or to try new procedures. His sometimes unorthodox approach and spirit of adventure had won him that reputation for brilliance as a neuro-surgeon, she knew.

It seemed to Jenefer that Blake had the Midas touch. Everything he touched seemed to turn to gold for him. He had won acclaim as a medical student, both at university and at Hartlake, and when they first met he was already tipped for an eventual consultancy. Clever, attractive, a dedicated surgeon with a charismatic degree of charm, everything he had ever wanted had fallen into his hands.

Including herself.

But the woman of today was a different person from yesterday's girl who had fallen head over heels in love with an ambitious surgeon. First love had swept into her life to fill heart and mind with rapturous dreams of happy ever after that she had been so sure he shared. But they had been shortlived dreams.

First love hadn't survived the double blows of rejection and bitter humiliation, and Jenefer was devoutly thankful that it could never come again. A girl learned to take better care of her heart after that kind of experience. Star surgeons seldom married romantic first-year nurses—but that was a lesson she had learned too late to save herself a lot of heartache.

'Sister . . .?'

Jenefer turned.

'It's Miss Hamilton, Sister. Nurse Walsh says can you come?'

Recalled to her duties by the urgency in the junior's voice, Jenefer hurried into the ward and whisked behind the curtains that were drawn about the old lady's bed.

The pulse was almost imperceptible and her breathing scarcely fluttered the thin chest. Brenda was having a little difficulty in replacing the old oxygen cylinder with a full one, and Jenefer went to her assistance.

They both expected the worst, but the frail old lady miraculously rallied and even managed to smile as gentle hands made her comfortable. 'So good,' she murmured. 'So kind. I give you young girls such a lot of trouble, I'm afraid. So sorry . . .'

Sister and staff nurse exchanged glances across the bed. Most patients were touchingly grateful to the nurses who looked after them day and night with such tender loving care. Miss Hamilton might look a sweet old lady, but she had an acid tongue and a carping nature and she had complained incessantly since admission. She had reduced the juniors to tears so often that eventually the task of nursing her had fallen to Jenefer and her senior staff nurse, who were hardened to difficult patients.

The praise was very welcome after days of criticism and complaint, but it was probably a sign that the old lady was failing fast, Jenefer thought wryly. There was no one to inform, for she seemed to have neither family nor friends nor interested neighbours.

For an awful moment, Jenefer saw herself at eighty-three, old and sick, unloved and unwanted, bitterly recalling an unsatisfactory love affair of long ago and realising that years of dedicated nursing had left her lonely and unfulfilled.

She loved her job. But she didn't want it to be all there was to her life.

CHAPTER THREE

THE GLASS doors guarding entrance and exit of Main Hall opened automatically at Jenefer's approach and she emerged into a pleasant evening after a long day on the ward when she had had little time to think of anything but work. There was a chilly breeze beneath the April sunshine and she drew her coat more closely about her shoulders as she headed for the staff car park. She turned at a light touch on her arm, her heart leaping. But it was only her newest junior who had hurried to catch up with her.

'Excuse me, Sister,' Ann said breathlessly. 'You went to Penfold High, didn't you? I'm sure I remember you as a prefect.'

Jenefer's lovely smile burgeoned. 'Oh, heavens—pigtailed and po-faced,' she laughed. 'I hoped I'd changed out of all recognition!' She looked curiously at the other girl. 'I don't remember you, I'm afraid . . .'

'I was only there for one term.' To satisfy her father's socialist instincts, Ann thought dryly. Then her mother had persuaded him to send her to an expensive private school. 'I was a fourth-form rebel who spent much of my time outside the Head's door, awaiting punishment for my sins. You sent me there on several occasions, actually.'

'Did I? You must be a reformed character, or you wouldn't have been accepted for nurse training,' Jenefer pointed out lightly.

'Or teacher training!'

'Didn't you like teaching?'

'Not really. I wanted to nurse, but my mother talked me out of it. She said I wasn't tough enough. No one warned me that I'd need to be a whole lot tougher to handle a class of five-year-old tearaways! I still bear the scars!' Ann grinned. 'I wasn't a very good teacher. I hope to be a much better nurse,' she said frankly.

'You seem to enjoy the work and you get on well with the patients,' Jenefer encouraged, hunting for car keys in her shoulder bag. 'You live out, don't you? Do you have transport? If not, I can give you a lift as far as the High Street, if it helps . . .?' Usually she kept a slight distance between herself and the juniors, but she rather liked the warmth and sparkle of Ann Morley, in spite of one or two reservations.

'I do have a car, but it's in for a minor repair. Thanks for the offer, but I'm being picked up by a friend this evening . . .' Ann underlined the words with a wave for the man who stood beside a gleaming silver Jaguar, hand resting lightly on the roof, a smile of welcome in his eyes.

Jenefer felt a shock of surprise. Then, recalling the way that the first-year had smiled at the surgeon that morning, arousing all her suspicions, she wondered why she was so astonished. For wasn't it typical of Blake to follow up an obvious invitation so promptly? Ann Morley was a pretty, confident extrovert. Just his type!

She slid behind the wheel of her small Fiat as the surgeon put an arm about Ann Morley and kissed her, smiling down at her like an old friend or a long-time lover. The secret of his success with women had always been a gift for making every woman feel that she was 'special', Jenefer thought with a stab of bitterness, observing the glow in the girl's pretty face in response to that warm welcome.

Like many dark men, Blake had a fondness for blondes. To this day, Jenefer didn't know why *she* had been singled out for notice, with her chestnut curls and hazel eyes. But it had been a shortlived fancy, in any case. Whatever else had changed, it seemed that his taste in women was consistent, she thought dryly. For it had been his relationship with a blonde physiotherapist at Hartlake that had ended their ill-starred engagement.

Now, within days of his arrival at Pagett's, he was apparently in pursuit of yet another blonde. Inserting the key in the ignition, Jenefer shrugged slim shoulders. She no longer cared what he did. It was a long time since Blake Armstrong had been important to her happiness, she reminded herself with pride.

Blake glanced across as she started the car. Then, with a word to his companion, he strode towards the Fiat with a purposeful light in his dark eyes. A startled Jenefer was tempted to drive away, cutting him dead, but that would only lead to the kind of speculation that she was anxious to avoid, she told herself sensibly.

She wound down the car window, eyeing him warily.

Blake lowered his tall frame to speak to her, smiling. 'Are you in a hurry, Jenefer? Ann and I are going over the road for a drink. Why don't you come with us?'

The casual friendliness of the invitation took her breath away. There was a beguiling warmth in the dark eyes, sweet persuasion in his enchanting smile, and he spoke as if those six years had never happened. Jenefer hardened her heart and her resolve, marvelling at his apparent ability to forget. The heartache and humiliation of their last encounter were indelibly stamped on *her* memory, and now she was unmoved by the hint of a dangerous charm. Her heart was protected by indifference rather than the angry ice he seemed to think he could melt with the warmth of his smile.

She looked at him, coolly amused. 'A girl on each arm? That sounds just like you, Blake. Thanks—but no, thanks!'

'We've a lot of news to catch up on,' he pressed lightly. 'And I gather you and Ann went to the same school at one time, so you've something else in common.'

She wondered what he meant by '*something else*'— nursing . . . or himself? 'You won't endear yourself if you drag former girlfriends along on your dates, as I surely don't need to tell you,' she said dryly. 'It isn't like you to be so clumsy.'

A frown etched itself between the surgeon's eyes. 'How can you possibly know what is or isn't like me after so long? People change, Jenefer.'

She shrugged. 'Some things never change. But I really can't pretend to be interested.' She released the handbrake. 'Stand back, Blake—I don't want to crush your toes.'

'Merely my ego?' he suggested with the glint of a wry smile.

'Your ego could probably do with crushing. You always were insufferably conceited, and that's one thing that doesn't appear to have changed at all!'

Glancing in the car mirror as she drove off, Jenefer saw that Blake's smile had deepened in response to the tart words and she wondered crossly what he found to amuse him in the situation.

For her part, she found it unwelcome and embarrassing. But it was typical of Blake to take it all so lightly. It hadn't been *his* heart that had come close to breaking all those years ago! No doubt she ought to be grateful to him for turning up again and proving to her satisfaction at least that he no longer meant anything. The might-have-been could haunt a girl's heart and mind at times when she felt low or a little lonely. But now she knew that she was content with the way things had turned out and that it was a relief to be free at last of a long-ago love.

Perhaps now she could give love a second chance . . .

On the way home, Jenefer stopped at a local supermarket for groceries and something special for dinner as well as some of the things she would need for Lucy's party later in the week. She liked to cook and she knew that her friend was relying on her to help out with the catering. They would need to supply plenty of food, for Lucy's parties tended to snowball!

It was almost six when she let herself in to the ground-floor flat of an elderly villa just off Penfold's High Street, home since her mother had remarried and moved to a nearby seaside town to run a small nursing home with her new husband. Staff nurse in theatres at the time, Jenefer had promptly applied to rent one of the flats in the newly converted house that belonged to a local chartered accountant.

Tom Cornell had subsequently become friend as well as landlord. His office was less than ten minutes' walk away, and it had been some weeks before Jenefer realised that the frequent visits from her new landlord to see how she was settling in were the prelude to courtship. She had naïvely supposed he was just being solicitous.

They had become close friends and Tom was coming to dinner that evening. Jenefer was looking forward to recounting the weekend's adventures, for he had met her scatterbrained sister and sympathised whenever she had to rush to the rescue yet again. He was due at seven, so there was no time to waste, and Jenefer didn't even pause to look at the mail she scooped up from the mat just inside the front door, although she recognised an early birthday card among the letters.

She had bought chicken and herbs and French bread and some wine for their evening meal. When everything was ready except for the finishing touches, she hurried to shower and dress, putting on a silk jersey dress of a gold that matched the flecks in her hazel eyes. She swept shining chestnut curls into a bunch that she secured with a gold butterfly clasp. Gold hooped ear-rings and a twisted gold rope about her neck completed the ensemble, just as the doorbell resounded through the flat.

Jenefer paused for a last glance in the mirror, approving her reflection, and banished the disloyal thought that Tom wouldn't appreciate the pains she had taken to look nice for him. He was not given to noticing or to paying compliments, she thought wryly. In fact, he wasn't a romantic or sentimental man. She was used to his prosaic attitude, but there were moments when she longed for some enthusiastic wooing and had to remind herself that she encouraged Tom simply because he could be trusted not to sweep her off her feet.

She could rely on him to be punctual and to bring her flowers too, she thought gratefully, burying her nose in their scented faces.

'They're lovely, Tom!'

He held her at arms' length and looked her over critically. 'I can see that you had an exhausting weekend with your sister. The strain is showing, I'm afraid.'

Jenefer smiled. 'Oh, it wasn't too bad,' she demurred, lifting her face for the customary kiss, cool lips glancing off her cheek.

She was used to the reserved and rather chilly courtship that didn't seem to mind her own lack of real response. Blake's tempestuous assault on her heart and senses had swept her into loving that led nowhere, and as a result she welcomed the unhurried and undemanding relationship with a man who *hadn't* talked of marrying her within days of first meeting and then cried off.

Tom might take his time to weigh up all the considerations, but he was reliable and kind and *safe*. Jenefer felt she might be persuaded to marry him in time, for *he* wouldn't expect her to give up nursing to become a full-time wife. He understood what her job meant to her and *he* had applauded her promotion to Ward Sister. His understanding and admiration and encouragement had gone a long way towards healing wounds inflicted by a very different man, in fact.

Tom carried his drink into the kitchen. 'How was the weekend, anyway? Did the move go off all right?' He lifted the lid of the stewpot to cast a critical eye over the simmering contents. He opened the fridge door to check if she had remembered the wine and tested the crusty newness of the loaf that lay ready to be cut.

'Do you want a synopsis or will you wait to read the book?' Jenefer laughed. She ought to be used to the way he took over in her kitchen, but for some reason his superior air was vaguely irritating to her that evening. He was a much better cook than herself and he didn't mean to offend, she told herself firmly. It was just Tom being Tom.

'Then it was an eventful few days?'

'It was certainly eventful! Everything that could go wrong did, of course! They hadn't even begun to pack when I arrived. Jocelyn was sitting on an empty tea-chest, sketching the baby as she shared her cereal with the dog!' She sighed. 'I just wish she wasn't quite so disorganised at times.'

'Why should she bother to be anything else when she knows that you'll walk in and take over and have everything under control in minutes? You're a very capable person, Jenefer.'

'I suppose so . . .' It didn't seem like a compliment. Capable was probably just another word for bossy, she thought ruefully.

Jenefer Gale, capable school prefect, capable Ward Sister, capable organiser of her sister's haphazard affairs—but not so clever at running her own life or she would never have made the mistakes that had cost her the man she loved.

Listening to gossip and challenging Blake, losing her temper and hurling her engagement ring at him, allowing pique and pride to drive her from Hartlake so there was no chance of a reconciliation. If she had been less hasty, Blake's interest in that other girl might have fizzled out and they might have married, after all.

Jenefer thrust the thought of Blake from her mind. His presence at Pagett's had cast a shadow over the day. She wasn't going to let him spoil her evening too!

Over dinner, she gave an amusing account of the weekend, careful to devalue her major role in solving each problem as it arose, for she didn't want credit for doing her best for Jocelyn. She had been doing that for as long as she could remember!

Tom listened and smiled and suggested that it was time Jocelyn stood on her own feet instead of relying on Jenefer to come to the rescue every time. She knew he was right, but she felt a prickle of resentment.

He was very thin, almost gaunt, but he had an excellent appetite. 'Very good,' he approved, pushing away his plate. 'Perhaps a little less basil . . .?'

'I'll remember.' Jenefer swallowed irritation, wondering why she was so unusually touchy about his well-meant culinary advice. She smiled at him. 'There's gateau with fresh cream,' she offered.

Tom shook his head. 'Nothing sweet for me,' he reproved. 'It ruins the palate.' He drank the last of his wine and got to his feet. 'I'll make the coffee, shall I? It was slightly too weak last time.'

'You know where the things are.' Jenefer swept dishes from the table and carried them out to the kitchen before she was tempted to throw something at him. She must be tired or pre-menstrual, for she wasn't usually so impatient with Tom. But was he always so pompous, so patronising, and she simply hadn't noticed before—or had she fallen into the dangerous trap of comparing him with another man?

Tom and Blake Armstrong were chalk and cheese—and she knew which of them she would rather trust with her happiness, she told herself firmly.

'I can't take you to Lucy's party, after all,' Tom announced as he carefully spooned coffee into the percolator. 'A client wants me to handle his tax assessment and he won't trust any papers to the post. So it means a trip to the Lake District and I shall be away for a few days, I'm afraid.'

Jenefer was disappointed. She didn't mind so much about the party, but she had hoped that he would take her out for a small celebration on her birthday. He had made no mention of the day and she wondered if he had forgotten.

'He's a special client,' Tom went on. 'A writer who lived locally until he lost his wife. When he moved North, I thought he'd take his tax problems with him, but I've taken care of them for so long that he probably trusts me to make sense of them. He's invited me to stay, so I shall be able to combine business with some pleasure . . . golf, fishing, some good walks and all that splendid scenery.'

'Sounds lovely.' Jenefer sounded wistful, for the Lake District was a favourite place, filled with memories of happy family holidays in the past.

'I wish I could take you along.' Tom rested a hand on her shoulder as she stood at the sink, immersing dishes in warm, soapy water to soak.

For some reason, Jenefer didn't believe the smooth words. She had never doubted him before, but she was suddenly convinced that the last thing Tom would want was her company on the proposed trip. 'I daren't take any more time off just now,' she returned lightly, taking his words at face value.

'I knew that's what you'd say if I suggested it. I can't compete with your work,' he teased. 'But perhaps we can arrange something for next month—if Pagett's and your sister and your numerous friends can spare you! By the way, I believe you have a detailed map of the Lakes? May I borrow it, Jenefer? Pettifer lives in a rather remote spot about five miles outside Windermere and it might help me to locate his house before nightfall!'

'Of course. I haven't seen it for some time, but I

expect I can find it for you . . .' Jenefer dried her hands and went into the living-room, leaving Tom in charge of the bubbling percolator.

Kneeling to search for the map in a low cupboard, she came across a half-forgotten box. She sank back on her heels, rather shaken by a coincidence that had brought it to light on the very day that Blake Armstrong had walked back into her life.

She lifted the lid to reveal a clutter of letters and photos and theatre programmes and other souvenirs that she had hidden away, clinging to them out of sentiment, although she had been quite unable to look at them again all these years.

She turned over a once-treasured snapshot and Blake's handsome face leapt up at her, smiling and self-assured and once so dear that her heart contracted. She bundled the photograph back with everything else and hastily thrust the box out of sight as Tom came into the room with the tray.

'Any luck?'

Jenefer scrambled to her feet, wondering if she was as flushed as she felt. 'Sorry! It'll turn up when I'm not looking for it, of course. Somebody's law, isn't it?' she said brightly.

It was absurd to feel so guilty, but she had never told Tom about that long-ago engagement, and it would be difficult now to explain why she had kept it a secret from someone who loved her and wanted to marry her.

'Too late for me, I'm afraid. I'll look out for one at a motorway service station on my way. Don't bother to look any more, Jenefer.' Tom patted the sofa cushions at his side in smiling invitation as he relaxed, long legs outstretched. 'Come and pour the coffee and tell me everything that's happened on the ward today.'

Jenefer was dismayed to notice that her hands weren't quite steady as she poured coffee and handed his cup. It was silly to be so affected by reminders of a youthful romance, she scolded herself sternly. After all, she had got over it long ago.

As a layman, Tom enjoyed hearing about a busy medical ward and the problems of its patients, and there were times when Jenefer wondered if she allowed him to play such a big part in her private life simply because he wasn't a doctor. Since Blake, she had kept all doctors at a distance.

Knowing that he was interested in Hilda Maitland, she mentioned that surgery was contemplated. 'Ryan has called in a neuro-surgeon to advise in her case—a newcomer to Pagett's. He's a Hartlake man, actually,' she added, feeling a strange kind of compulsion to bring Blake into the conversation.

Tom knew that she had originally trained at the famous hospital in London, but she had never told him very much about her experiences. 'One of your former colleagues, then?' he suggested with a smile.

'Scarcely!' she disclaimed. 'I never set foot in a theatre at Hartlake. I was a very junior dogsbody and dutifully kept my eyes glued to the floor whenever a surgeon crossed my path. They were gods to us first-years!' Her tone was bright, but her face grew warm as she uttered the evasive words.

'So you don't know this man at all?'

'Hartlake is a big place, Tom. I couldn't possibly have known every doctor and surgeon on the staff—and, as a junior nurse, I was practically invisible to most of them, in any case,' she told him firmly, already regretting the impulse that had led her to mention Blake. She went on to talk about some of the other patients on Cresswell.

Old Miss Hamilton, fighting a losing battle for life.
Mrs Wilcox, whose sense of humour was helping her
to come to terms with the ravages of kidney disease.
The sixteen-year-old admitted with pneumonia and
pleurisy as a result of walking miles to her home in a
thunderstorm after quarrelling with her boyfriend—a
girl with a pride to match her own, Jenefer thought
wryly, remembering the torrential rain on a certain
memorable night in her own life.

Tom rose to leave earlier than usual, and she looked
at him in surprise. 'I've some papers that I must look
through and some packing to do, and I'm sure you'll
welcome an early night.' Taking her hands, he drew
her up and into a light, undemanding embrace.

Jenefer stood in the circle of his arms, tilting her
head to look up at him, for he was very tall, taller even
than Blake, a lean man with ascetic good looks. She
felt a flicker of familiar panic. They weren't lovers,
but she was sure that Tom would like them to be. She
wasn't ready for that degree of commitment and, so
far, he had accepted the limits that she set to their
relationship without apparent resentment. But even
his patience must eventually wear thin, she felt.

She might have believed herself frigid and worried
about it, but the fierce flame of passion just as much
as love had urged her into Blake's arms without
hesitation all those years ago. It seemed that her
longing for a man's lovemaking had to be two-
fold—and, nice though he was, much as she liked him,
she neither loved nor desired poor Tom.

Sensing the expected resistance in her slender
frame, Tom dropped a light kiss on her bunched curls
and let her go. 'I'm sorry about the party, Jenefer.
Make my excuses to Lucy, won't you?'

Still not a word about her birthday—and she had no

intention of reminding him, Jenefer thought proudly.

'I'm sorry you'll miss it. But Lucy's parties aren't really your scene, are they?' She knew he was only invited because her friends thought of them as a couple who would eventually marry. It pleased Tom and she didn't correct the assumption because it kept other men at bay.

When Tom had gone, promising to telephone her from Windermere, Jenefer wondered if she was in danger of marrying a man she didn't love because she dreaded the pain and possible disappointment of loving anyone again. But where was the risk in marrying someone who really cared for her and would do all he could to make her happy? She was puzzled by her continued reluctance to take a step that she had once contemplated with such breathless excitement. There was far more security in Tom's love than Blake had ever offered. In any case, she didn't think it was possible to know again that 'first fine careless rapture' of her feeling for Blake. Surely that only came with youth and hope and dreaming?

Perhaps a different kind of love would come along if she married Tom and did her best to make him a good wife. It was some time since he had broached the subject and she knew he was waiting for her to make up her mind. She was grateful for his patience and his understanding. She was very, very fond of him. But she was still a long way from chancing her happiness.

Or Tom's.

CHAPTER FOUR

JENEFER stood at the open drugs trolley, slim and trim in her dark blue, organza cuffs about her rolled sleeves, waiting for her senior staff nurse to check a dosage against the patient's chart. At a nod from Brenda, she shook two more capsules from a bottle into a tiny plastic container and gave it to the staff nurse to take to Hilda.

'She's very popular today, isn't she?' Brenda observed on her return, indicating the young doctor who had drawn a chair to the side of Hilda's bed and was earnestly taking notes.

'She's loving every moment of it too,' said Jenefer, smiling. She had expected Hilda to be bewildered and confused by the succession of visitors: Blake's houseman, his anaesthetist, a phlebotomist requiring blood samples, an unknown physiotherapist, young doctors wanting to write up her case, porters to take her for more X-rays or yet another brain scan. Instead, she seemed to be revelling in the interest that was taken in her since Blake's visit.

The surgeon had ordered a number of tests to be carried out and the results rushed through, but he had apparently delegated his interest in the case to Barry Rowe, his junior registrar, who had been to see Hilda that morning and informed Jenefer that his boss had a heavy surgical list and no time to visit Cresswell.

Jenefer had been relieved, for it meant that she could get on with her work without constantly looking over her shoulder for a sight of the surgeon. His

arrival at Pagett's had caused so much talk and
excitement among the nurses that she could only
marvel that she hadn't been aware of his appointment
to the NSU before he walked into her ward. Now it
seemed to her that his name was constantly being
mentioned, a perpetual reminder of his presence—and
the past. Jenefer found it very irritating.

As though she had read the Ward Sister's mind,
Brenda commented on the surgeon's absence from the
ward. 'No sign of the charmer, is there?'

'The charmer?' Jenefer echoed indifferently as she
trundled the drugs trolley towards the next patient.
'Who's that?'

'Why, Blake Armstrong, of course! That's what the
juniors call him. Didn't you know? It's that smile.
Haven't you noticed the way it lights up his whole
face?'

'I've noticed that the juniors seem to have nothing
better to do than talk and giggle about him whenever
two of them get together,' Jenefer returned tartly.
'You and I are past all that nonsense, I hope!' She
flicked over the Kardex. 'Mrs Savage. No further
medication.' She smiled at the beaming black woman
who sat on the edge of her bed, fully dressed and
clutching her handbag, eagerly watching the swing
doors of the ward. 'Waiting for your husband, Evie?'

'That's right, Sister. My George is coming to take
me home right now!'

'We shall miss you. Won't we, Nurse Walsh?'

'Yes, indeed. You've brightened the ward with that
lovely laugh of yours,' Brenda agreed, giving Evie a
hug. '*And* kept us all supplied with sweeties to keep us
going!'

Evie chuckled. 'I'm coming to see you all next
month when I visit Dr Montague's clinic,' she

promised. 'And I'll bring you girls a big box of sweeties to show I haven't forgotten everything you did for me!'

'Just bring yourself, Evie. We'll be pleased to see you,' Jenefer assured her warmly, but she suspected that the woman would either forget or feel uncomfortable about visiting the ward and taking the nurses away from their routines if only for a few minutes. Patients soon forgot their attachment to the nurses who looked after them when they were sick and dependent. It was natural and healthy that the bond should break on discharge, and patients were forgotten sooner than they would like to believe by busy nurses. Beds were filled almost immediately and there was always someone else in need of the caring and compassion that had brought each of them into nursing.

It certainly wasn't the hours. Or the pay. Or a liking for responsibility and hard work, Jenefer thought dryly as she and Brenda went on with the drugs round.

But if nursing was in a girl's blood then it seemed that nothing, not long hours or poor pay or the drudgery of routine ward work, could make her give up the profession. Even marriage and motherhood couldn't keep a dedicated nurse from the wards for long. Many Pagett's nurses had husbands and children but worked night shifts or put in whatever hours they could during the day to ease the chronic staff shortage at the general hospital that served a large area with a growing population.

A little later, Jenefer was writing up the ward report when a familiar tattoo sounded on the glass of the open office door. She put down her pen and smiled as Ryan came into the room.

'Sorry to disturb you at one of your favourite occupations, Sister!' he teased.

She laughed. 'I'd rather talk to you than fill forms,' she assured him warmly. 'Would you like some tea, or is this an official visit?'

'No tea, thanks. I can only spare a minute or two . . .' He perched on the corner of her desk in spite of the warning—a busy doctor, like overworked nurses, learned to snatch every opportunity for rest. 'Actually, I'm looking for Armstrong.'

'I don't think he's on the ward . . .' She schooled the heart that had an alarming tendency to leap at the mention of the surgeon's name.

'A man that size isn't easy to miss,' Ryan said dryly.

Collaboration with the neuro-surgeon had evidently done nothing to dispel an initial dislike, Jenefer thought ruefully. 'Have you tried Theatres? I understood he'd be operating for most of the day.'

'He finished his list over an hour ago and left.'

'I see.' Jenefer was slightly surprised—and possibly disappointed—that Blake hadn't made a point of visiting his patient on Cresswell. Maybe he had simply gone home—wherever that was these days. Or to the pub. Or the local golf club. Or sailing. After a heavy list, most surgeons liked to unwind and relax in a favourite pursuit.

'I want to talk to him about Hilda's tests. Most of the results are through and it looks as if he'll definitely have to operate—the sooner the better from the patient's point of view, and I don't think he can argue about that. You'll come along to Theatres to see the great man in action, no doubt?'

'I'm not sure.'

'Try to make it,' Ryan urged. 'He's said to be a brilliant surgeon. Frankly, I wonder why he came to

Pagett's when he could have commanded a consultancy almost anywhere in the world.'

It was a puzzle to Jenefer too. 'Perhaps Pagett's—or Penfold—holds an attraction for him that we don't know about.'

He seized on an unintended implication. 'A woman, do you mean? A Pagett's nurse, perhaps? I saw him in the Winchester the other evening with that blonde first-year from this ward—what's her name? Marley?'

'I expect you mean Ann Morley.'

'That's the one!' Ryan ran a hand through the thick waves of his own blond hair. 'They had their heads very close together, talking nineteen to the dozen, smiling into each other's eyes. Old friends, are they?'

'I've no idea.' Firmly, Jenefer closed her mind to the image of intimacy that the words conjured up.

'She's well into her twenties, surely? What was she doing before she became a nurse?' he asked curiously.

'Teaching at a primary school in London.'

'London? So it's possible that she and Armstrong knew each other before either of them came to this part of the world?'

'Very likely.' Jenefer picked up her pen to indicate that she was too busy to discuss the affairs of surgeon or first-year nurse. She wondered if Ryan had taken one of his fancies to the girl. It would explain his persistent interest. He was probably wasting his time, for it was very obvious that Ann Morley had other fish to fry, she thought dryly.

Her heart had sunk at the suggestion that Blake might have followed the girl to Pagett's. Deeply in love, had he sacrificed the long-awaited consultancy to follow his heart?

'I wonder if she'd like to go to Lucy's party? Meet some people, make some friends . . . what do you think? Shall I ask her?'

'I think she's the type to enjoy a party for any reason,' said Jenefer, encouraging his interest in the girl. 'But I expect she'll know some of the people there, in any case. She's a local girl, Ryan.'

'Is she?' A thought struck him. 'Not one of *the* Morleys?'

It hadn't occurred to Jenefer to connect Ann with the wealthy family who seemed to own most of Penfold and the surrounding district. She smiled at the unlikely thought that a Morley would choose to earn her own living as a nurse. 'I doubt it,' she said dryly.

'So do I. I couldn't be that lucky,' said Ryan, his eyes dancing.

'She must be one of the few local girls that you've missed,' Jenefer teased, for his girlfriends had been legion in the years that she had known him. *She* had never been one of them, however.

He grinned. 'Perhaps that should be remedied—and there's no time like the present!' With a gleam in his bright blue eyes, he turned to the door.

'Not now!' Jenefer's mock-stern tone stopped him in his tracks. 'You know the rules! No flirting on my ward, Dr Montague!'

'What a martinet you turned out to be!' he groaned.

She laughed. 'I need to be to protect my nurses from marauding medics!'

'And who protects the protector?'

'Oh, I can look after myself,' Jenefer assured him confidently.

'Too well, perhaps! Starch every day keeps the doctors at bay!'

'And that's just the way I want it.'

Ryan regarded her thoughtfully. 'I remember the

old days, Jenefer, when you had so many men on a string that there was never room for me. What happened?'

Blake happened, she thought wryly. Ever since, she had been wary of men. Ryan was as ignorant of that long-ago engagement as most of her friends and she wasn't tempted to confide in him now. Besides, there was no point in furthering his obvious dislike of a new colleague.

'The string broke and they all fell off,' she said lightly.

'So you've settled for Tom Cornell.' It was statement rather than question, faintly disapproving.

Jenefer frowned. 'I haven't settled for anyone yet,' she objected. 'Tom's just a friend.' She didn't want Ryan or anyone else taking it for granted that she meant to marry Tom. Rumour ran riot at Pagett's!

'He's taking you to Lucy's party, I suppose?'

'Not this time. He's away on business.'

'Oh . . .' Ryan had seen Cornell's very distinctive Rolls heading out of town early one morning on a little used road, and although he wouldn't want to swear to it in a court of law he was pretty positive that the woman in the passenger seat had been Nicola Lomax, wife of the local MP. Maybe there was an innocent explanation and maybe he maligned the man, but he suspected that Cornell was up to funny business, in fact. He had no intention of saying so to the obviously unsuspecting Jenefer, however.

'He's gone to the Lake District to see a client,' Jenefer explained. 'But I shall be at the party, of course. Lucy couldn't manage without the head cook and bottle-washer!'

Ryan hesitated. 'Well, if you're stuck for someone to take you . . .'

Jenefer wasn't offended by the lack of compliment in that rather reluctant offer. 'That's very nice of you, Ryan. But I'm going early to organise the food and it will be easier to make my own way, thanks.'

'In that case, I probably will try my luck with Ann Morley. As soon as she's off duty.' On his way out of the room, Ryan paused to blow her a most unethical kiss. 'Oh, by the way—happy birthday, Sister!'

'I loved your card!' Jenefer called after him gratefully. It had been a hectic day on the ward, but she hadn't minded. Spending the day doing what she most enjoyed, teaching her nurses and caring for patients, was probably the ideal birthday, after all.

She'd had cards and gifts from family and friends. Patients had shyly offered small tokens throughout the day. Cresswell nurses and ancillary staff had clubbed together to buy her a silk scarf and some chocolates and people had popped into the ward or rung her up with their good wishes. It was almost embarrassing, but very heartwarming to know that she was so well liked, and it took the edge off her disappointment that Tom had forgotten.

It would have been very silly to expect Blake to remember . . .

Jenefer eyed the remaining pile of paperwork with distaste. She felt that her place was on the ward, helping nurses and reassuring patients and ensuring its smooth running. She hoped the sweeping changes promised for the Health Service would relieve her of some of the administrative work that took time that could be used in many other ways. With a sigh, she went on with the report.

It was still unfinished when a nurse came to the door, looking pale. It was the second of her new first-year nurses and she was obviously shaken and upset.

'Sister, could you have a look at Miss Hamilton, please? She's a funny colour . . .'

Instantly, Jenefer was on her feet and hurrying into the ward. She had expected the summons, but it was probably the first-year's first brush with death, and she paused to say kindly: 'Go and make yourself some tea, Nurse. I'll attend to Miss Hamilton.'

The old lady's passing cast a cloud. No nurse, however experienced, could be totally unmoved by death and the whole ward sensed its sobering presence. As soon as she could, Jenefer made a special round of the ward with a bright face and a cheerful word for every patient. Some were too ill or too drugged or too self-absorbed to have noticed the drawn curtains or the meaningful bustle of nurses and porters. But Hilda wasn't so tired or so confused by her busy day that she was immune to the import of the newly made-up bed that already awaited the next admission to the ward.

Clutching Jenefer, she jerked her head at the empty bed, tears running down her florid face and her mouth working. Across the pages of a child's exercise book she had scrawled her own name in huge, untidy letters, over and over again.

Jenefer put an arm about the heavy shoulders to give the big woman a comforting cuddle, aware of the dread that underlay the awkwardly written word. 'Not you, lovely. You'll be walking out of here to go home very soon.' Hilda mouthed a garbled protest. 'Yes, I know you're worried, but Mr Armstrong is a very clever surgeon and he wouldn't operate if there was any risk,' she said firmly, surreptitiously crossing her fingers. 'It will make you feel much better and soon you'll be able to do more for yourself, and you'll like that, I know. It might take time, but you'll show us all that you can make it!'

A star patient for a star surgeon, she felt with instinctive confidence in Blake. Perhaps it would take a miracle to restore Hilda's impaired faculties to any real extent. But Blake, like all surgeons, was in the miracle business.

Jenefer went off duty that evening with no plans to celebrate her birthday. Family and friends had assumed that she was spending the evening with Tom and she hadn't bothered to explain—and she had little heart for celebrating without him.

Instead, she began preparations for Lucy's party, baking vol-au-vents and quiches and sausage rolls, making a variety of cakes. When she had finished, she couldn't be bothered to cook for herself. She wasn't hungry.

She dawdled in a hot bath and then curled up on the sofa with a sandwich and a sausage roll and a mug of coffee to watch a television 'soap', but she found it hard to be interested in the adventures of make-believe lovers.

Her bored gaze roamed the room and fell on the cupboard that contained a box she had been refusing to think about for days. Suddenly it was drawing her like a magnet. There was no reason why she shouldn't look through its contents—and it was about time that she discarded most of them, she told herself sensibly. She was getting too old for silly sentiment, surely!

Switching off the television set, she sat on the carpet in her thin silk robe, still damp curls gleaming in the light from the lamp, and upturned the box. Out tumbled photos and letters and old bills, crumpled ticket stubs, the faded rose that she had pressed between the pages of a small, dog-eared diary; the invitation to a friend's wedding that had coupled their names for the first time and given her such a thrill of delight; the few hurried notes from a busy surgeon suggesting a meeting or ruefully cancelling an appointment—and the delicate silver bracelet that had been the very first gift from Blake and ought to have been returned to him along with her engagement ring.

Nothing worth keeping but the bracelet, Jenefer told herself firmly, and very little to mark the fact that in the space of a few short weeks two people had met and fallen in and out of love.

In the words of an old song, their love had been 'too hot not to cool down', a headlong slide towards the inevitable disappointment from breathtaking peaks of ecstatic optimism, she thought wryly, stroking the fragile links of the bracelet with a tentative finger, memory evoking the moment when Blake had clasped the lovely thing about her wrist.

The haunting recollection of his lingering touch was suddenly so vivid, so tactile, that a tremor shivered along her spine. Her heart filled with tears as she recalled the look in his dark eyes, the sweetness in his smile, the unforgettably tender intent in the way he took her into his arms.

She had loved him so much, so much . . .

Jenefer moistened suddenly dry lips, heart pounding and a familiar sinking in her stomach as she recalled the lovemaking that had followed. No other man had ever stirred her so strongly and she had given herself without any thought of holding back, loving him, trusting him, believing in the future they were meant to share.

It had been an incredible few weeks. Jenefer remembered very clearly that intoxicating excitement of heart and mind and body, coming close to madness and making it impossible for her to remain at Hartlake within inevitable sight and sound of the man who had abruptly decided that she wasn't a suitable wife after all. With an effort she thrust away the disturbing, painful memories.

His warmth, his tenderness, his loving words had all been lies, she thought bitterly. He had never understood that love had turned her life upside down and inside out so that nothing mattered but pleasing him, making him happy, being with him until the end of time. In return, he had hurt and disappointed her and let her down.

Well, she had learned not to make the same mistake again. Her heart had been her own since Blake threw it back and it might be a very long time before she gave it away again to any man!

She scrambled to silence the telephone as it shrilled across her chaotic thoughts. Tom! Ringing from the Lakes, as he'd promised—and on her birthday, too! Reliable, kindhearted, lovable Tom! 'Hallo . . .?'

'Voices don't change, do they?' Blake drawled in his own deep voice that had once thrilled her with its exciting timbre and apparently still had the power to quicken her heartbeat. 'Yours is instantly recognisable, Jenefer.'

'How did you get my home number?' she demanded, resenting the ease with which he expected to pick up the threads. Didn't he know that the fabric of their relationship had been ripped beyond repair? 'Oh, never mind! It obviously wasn't difficult. What do you want, Blake?'

'A warmer reception than that from an old friend, for one thing,' he said smoothly.

'I'm surprised that you expect anything at all from me, in the circumstances,' she said tartly. 'You're lucky that I even talk to you!'

'I know. You've a warm heart and a forgiving nature, my sweet.'

Jenefer stiffened, visualising the dance of his dark eyes as he uttered the mocking words. He had never taken anything seriously—least of all love! 'Don't be sarcastic!' she snapped.

Blake chuckled. 'Happy birthday, Jenefer. Why aren't you out celebrating with your friends?'

Her heart lurched. Had he really remembered? Or had someone reminded him? 'I fancied an evening at home.'

'Alone?'

'Why not?' she countered. 'Birthdays aren't so important at my age.'

'Poor old lady,' he teased softly. 'I'm in the pub on the corner. The Feathers, is it? Come and join me and we'll both cry into our beer for our lost youth.'

'I've better things to do . . .' But the snap of the words was lost in the buzz of a disconnected line, and Jenefer doubted that he'd even heard the angry rejection of something that could scarcely be called an invitation.

He hadn't waited for a reply. It was typical of a man who swept through life, crushing opposition with the sheer force of his charm, taking it for granted that every woman would dance to the magic of his tune. He didn't seem to understand that she wanted nothing more to do with him. So she would have to spell it out and then underline it for him—and why not right away?

Then there could be no doubt in anyone's mind that she really meant it!

CHAPTER FIVE

IT TOOK only moments to slip into a soft yellow skirt and matching shirt, to pull a comb through her curls and put on a splash of bright lipstick. Then, slipping key and purse into the pockets of her jaunty grey jacket, Jenefer set off on the short walk to the pub, determined to speak her mind and return home as soon as possible.

The Feathers was crowded and noisy with music and laughter and the hubbub of many voices. It was not one of her favourite haunts. Her searching glance immediately found Blake, standing at the bar, handsome and distinguished, aloof despite several hopeful glances from unattached women. He was the kind who attracted her sex like moths to a flame, Jenefer thought irritably as she squeezed through the crowd to reach him, and *her* wings had been badly singed. She had no intention of getting too close to him again.

Dark eyes swept her shining hair and slightly flushed face and met the militant sparkle of her hazel gaze. Blake smiled. 'I knew you wouldn't disappoint me,' he murmured.

'I wish I could say the same for you,' Jenefer said sweetly.

His smile deepened. 'Touché!' He picked up already ordered drinks from the bar. 'Shall we get out of the crush? There's a table in that corner that seems to be waiting for us. I've got you a dry Martini, by the way. I hope that's still your drink? But perhaps it ought to be champagne . . .'

'Meeting you again is no reason for a celebration in my book,' Jenefer threw over her shoulder as she stalked towards the table he had indicated, refusing to be flattered because he had remembered her taste in drinks after so long. He had been much too sure that she would run at his smoothly confident call, she thought crossly. Now that she was here, she wondered what on earth had prompted such a ridiculous impulse to join him in The Feathers. Did she want to give him the impression that she still had a soft spot for him, for heaven's sake?

'I was referring to your birthday,' Blake said mildly, sliding on to the padded seat opposite her and placing the drinks on the table.

'Oh . . .' She had snapped too soon and she was slightly discomfited. She shrugged. 'Being twenty-five is nothing to celebrate, either.'

'Or to regret, surely? It's never too late to change some things, but growing older isn't one of them,' he reminded her lightly. His gaze rested on her in warm admiration. 'Besides, you've grown more beautiful with each year since we met. You were a lovely girl. Now you're a very beautiful woman.'

Jenefer didn't trust that glib tongue or the glow in his dark eyes. 'Get to the point, Blake,' she said coldly.

'The point . . .?'

'Why you rang. Why you wanted to see me.'

'I've been trying to see you all day. It just didn't work out, for one reason or another—clinic this morning, a heavy theatre list, seeing relatives. When I finally managed to get along to Cresswell you'd just gone off duty. I couldn't let the day pass, could I?' His smile was warm, his tone caressing.

'It hasn't bothered you before,' she said sharply, dismayed by the tremble of her limbs and the flutter of excitement in her breast as their eyes met.

'I thought of you each year as the day came round, Jenefer. It was a special day for us, after all,' he said softly.

Jenefer had been trying not to remember. Her nineteenth birthday—a very special day for her, certainly. But she was surprised that Blake recalled it so well. It was the day he had said that he loved her, wanted to marry her. The day he had slipped the lovely bracelet on her wrist and kissed her so tenderly. The day she had discovered heaven on earth in his arms.

Damn him for bringing it all flooding back with his words, his smiles! Damn him for turning up again to torment her with the insidious appeal of his magnetism! Damn his dangerous charm! 'I don't know what you're talking about. Either your memory is better than mine or you're confusing me with some other girl,' she said with airy indifference. But a betraying colour rose slowly in her face and her fingers tightened on the stem of the glass that contained her untouched Martini.

There was a gleam of satisfaction in the surgeon's eyes. 'I have an excellent memory, and you were quite unforgettable.' He raised his glass to her in smiling salute. 'Many happy returns.'

Sensing a hidden meaning to the conventional words, Jenefer resented the smooth reference to an intimacy she had tried to erase from her mind. 'Thanks,' she said coldly.

As if unaware of the resentment behind that ungracious tone, Blake sat back and smiled at her warmly. 'This is very pleasant,' he approved. 'Just like it used to be.'

'Things are nothing like they used to be,' she returned swiftly, a warning light in her hazel eyes.

'They could be if you'd only stop glowering and give me one of your lovely smiles,' he coaxed with all of his considerable charm.

Her heart was unmoved. But her treacherous body quickened with sudden longing for his touch, his kiss, his embrace with all its remembered delight. The way things used to be . . .

Her mouth hardened. 'I'm not in a smiling mood, Blake. Frankly, I don't know why I came when I've nothing at all to say to you!'

The glow of his smile was reflected in his eyes, blinding her to the shadow of hurt in their depths. 'Then just sit back and enjoy your drink and let me do the talking,' he suggested smoothly.

'Sweet-talking, no doubt! You were always very good at that!'

'You liked to hear it once upon a time.'

'Once upon a time is apt! When I was still young enough to believe in fairy stories! I've grown up, Blake. You don't impress me any more.' Alarmed by his renewed impact on her emotions, she was stringent.

Blake was suddenly intent, dark eyes boring into her own. 'We said enough hurtful things to each other to last a lifetime, Jenefer. We've both changed, grown older and, let's hope, wiser, and I thought we might be friends. Do we have to be at odds just because things didn't work out for us? Can't we be adult about the situation?'

Jenefer felt effectively reproached by the quiet words. 'I suppose so,' she grudged. It was all very well for him, she thought bitterly. *He* hadn't been the injured party. *He* hadn't been hurt and let down and left to explain the humiliating absence of an engagement ring to family and friends!

'Then why shouldn't we meet for a drink or a meal occasionally? You're a link with old friends and past times—happier times, to be trite. I'm delighted that we've met again. It might even be destiny,' he added with a twinkle.

'I can do without destiny,' Jenefer said bluntly. 'I never wanted to see you again.'

Blake's narrowed gaze locked her own. 'Do you hate me that much?'

Jenefer swallowed a choke of emotion as she thought of how much she had *loved* him. More than he would ever know! He had been her life, her hopes and dreams, her future—and he had walked away from her without apology or apparent regret. He had hurt her badly. She had missed him terribly. Why should she forgive and forget now just because he expected it with all the infuriating arrogance of a star surgeon? How dared he even ask it of her!

Pride sent words spilling from her lips. 'Oh, I don't hate you, Blake,' she assured him brightly. 'You did me a favour, as things turned out. I'm very happy as Sister Cresswell and, knowing the kind of man you are, I can't imagine a worse fate for any woman than being Mrs Blake Armstrong.'

His face turned stormy. She saw the darkening of his eyes, the flare of his nostrils and the angry tensing of his jaw. Smouldering, he got to his feet so abruptly that he bumped the table, spilling some of his lager and almost overturning her Martini. Jenefer put out a hasty hand to save her glass. So did Blake. Their fingers brushed and recoiled.

Blake glowered. 'Fortunately, my wife took a

different view,' he said curtly, and spun on his heel to head for the exit, anger etched into every line of his tall frame.

Jenefer felt as if the floor had surged up to hit her in the face. Deep down, she had cherished a secret dream that one day Blake would come in search of her to declare that he still loved her and had never found anyone to take her place in his heart or his life. When he begged her to marry him, she would delight in saying no and sending him away, of course. Then, later, she would relent . . .

So she was devastated to learn that at some time in the past six years, some other woman had swept an apparently determined bachelor to the altar, succeeding where she had failed.

She felt she could have forgiven him almost anything but that final blow to her pride.

After a bad night, she arrived on Cresswell to find the ward in an uproar because Hilda wanted the breakfast she wasn't allowed that morning. Her heartrending wails echoed along the corridor, and Jenefer hurried to calm the poor woman, so childlike in her distress and confusion. It was one of Hilda's bad days, and no one could make her understand that she wasn't allowed to eat anything because she was listed for surgery.

Jenefer managed to soothe her to some extent, but tears then gave way to scowling resentment. It was so unlike Hilda who did her best to smile in the face of terrible odds that Jenefer knew she must be terrified of the operation she was about to undergo.

Blake was expected to pay a routine visit to his patient that morning, and Jenefer hoped he would be able to set Hilda's mind at rest. She arranged for advance warning of his arrival so that she wouldn't be surprised into smiling at the surgeon. She was still furious with him.

Shocked by the sudden, swamping tide of his anger and shaken by the revelation of his words, embarrassed by curious glances, some sympathetic and some frankly amused, she had hastily made her own escape from The Feathers to hurry home, seething, knowing she had only herself to blame.

She ought to have ignored that peremptory summons. Instead, she had invited further humiliation as well as public speculation—and if she had known that Blake was a married man nothing on earth would have taken her to The Feathers to meet him!

She was puzzled that something so vital as the new surgeon's marital state had escaped the juniors, and she marvelled at Blake's apparent indifference to gossip. Rumour travelled at the speed of light and she had seen more than one familiar face in the pub. As Sister Cresswell, she was naturally well known, and Blake was a very distinctive newcomer, with his impressive height and magnificent good looks. She could imagine what was already being whispered about them on the wards and she didn't want any of it to get back to his unsuspecting wife. Jenefer knew just how much it hurt to love a man who couldn't be trusted. It must be a hundred times worse to be married to him!

She was writing out a discharge certificate for a doctor's signature when a junior nurse put her head round the open office door. 'Excuse me, Sister. You wanted to know as soon as Mr Armstrong arrived. He's just walked into the ward.'

'Thank you, Nurse.' Jenefer laid down her pen and shot her cuffs, steeling herself. When Blake appeared, dwarfing the doorway, she had the impression that he had wiped his very attractive smile from his handsome face only seconds before. 'Good morning, Mr Armstrong,' she said crisply.

His nod was cursory. 'I thought I ought to have a few words with Mrs Maitland before she has her pre-med, Sister. I expect she's feeling anxious this morning.'

'She isn't so much anxious as cross.'

'Throwing tantrums?' Blake knew and warmly sympathised with the many frustrations of stroke victims and there was no hint of criticism in his deep voice.

'She wants to know why she can't have her breakfast and why she has to wear a special gown and socks and why she can't go home—and she isn't listening to any of the answers.'

His smile was so slight as to be non-existent. 'I'll go along and have a chat with her. Perhaps she'll listen to me. I can see that you're busy, so I won't interrupt your work, Sister. I know my way.'

'I'm not at all busy.' Jenefer's firm tone checked the surgeon in mid-turn. She rose from the desk, skirts swishing. 'Mrs Maitland may not recognise you this morning. She's confused and upset and any unknown face alarms her at the moment. So I'd better come with you.'

Blake was as frigid as herself, confining his remarks to the subject of his patient as they made their way along the ward. Jenefer was in no doubt that he was still annoyed with her after last night's encounter. Well, she had meant her words, she thought defiantly. She *was* thankful that they had never married. In fact, feeling all the frost of his manner that morning, she was finding it hard to recall what she had ever seen in him apart from his good looks and rampant masculinity!

It was a relief to realise that she wouldn't see much of him in the weeks ahead. Chance had decreed that Ryan should ask the new neuro-surgical registrar to advise on Hilda's case, and it was an unkind quirk of fate that he had turned out to be Blake. But Hilda would be taken to another ward for specialised after-care when she left the Recovery Room later that day and there would be no further need or reason for Blake to visit Cresswell. Their paths might cross occasionally, but he was unlikely to pursue an initial attempt to renew their friendship now that she had offended him so effectively.

And that was just the way she wanted it!

His smiling charm was much in evidence as he reached for Hilda's chart to run a seemingly casual eye over its columns. 'This is the big day, Hilda,' he said lightly. Despite medication, her blood pressure was higher than he could wish. John Randall, his anaesthetist, was confident that he could handle the extra element of risk, however.

Hilda gave a small, despairing groan and tossed her head from side to side in angry frustration, clawing the air as she struggled to articulate some meaningful sounds. Her other hand, useless since the stroke and turned in on itself, lay limply on the coverlet.

Blake sat on the side of the bed and took the agitated hand into a reassuring clasp. 'Not feeling too good? Or too sure about the future? I can understand that,' he sympathised. 'But we're going to do our best for you and I don't want you to worry about a thing.' He smiled at her warmly. 'Now let me tell you again just what we're going to do for you this morning . . .'

Hilda's gaze never left the surgeon's handsome

face as he patiently explained all over again exactly what the operation entailed and what they hoped it would achieve, although he knew that much of what he said was beyond her present understanding.

Jenefer's newly hardened heart came close to softening as she listened to his deep, kind voice and observed the genuine warmth of his concern. She had known many doctors in her years of nursing. Sometimes, after many years of hospital work, the bedside manner wore a little thin. Sometimes it was slightly rushed or too obviously professional or so impersonal that it chilled. Patients could feel dismissed, unimportant, at a time when they most needed to feel that their problem was of paramount importance and interest to the doctor in charge of their case.

Blake's manner conveyed that he had all the time in the world for a very special patient that he was totally committed to curing, and Jenefer saw that Hilda responded to the flattering warmth of that obviously genuine interest. And, like so many women, she seemed to respond just as instinctively to the surgeon's charm and physical attractions.

'Sister is going to give you an injection very soon and that will make you feel less anxious about what's going to happen to you. And both Dr Randall and I will be on hand to look after you when you get to Theatres,' Blake assured his patient with a final pat of her hand as he rose to leave.

Hilda made an anxious clutch at his sleeve and raised herself from the pillows on a stream of mostly unintelligible words. She was so obviously agitated that Blake turned to Jenefer with an enquiring arch of a dark brow.

'What's the problem, Sister?' he asked, knowing

that she was much more familiar than himself with the needs and anxieties of her patients and probably attuned to that struggling speech.

Jenefer took a tissue from the box on the locker and gently wiped Hilda's wet mouth. 'No problem, really,' she said brightly. 'Hilda wants me to look after her while she's in the theatre and I said that I would. She wants to know if you object.'

'It seems a splendid idea,' Blake said pleasantly.

His smile might soothe and reassure his patient, but it didn't convince Jenefer that the suggestion had really met with his approval. She had seen the flicker of something very like irritation in his dark eyes, she thought, as she brushed greying strands of hair from Hilda's brow.

'There! That eases your mind, doesn't it?' she suggested warmly, and Hilda smiled her sadly twisted smile in reply.

Jenefer hurried to catch up with the surgeon, who was striding down the ward with the air of a man in a hurry. She could sense the wave of annoyance that emanated from him. Ward Sisters were seldom welcome in a busy operating theatre. But she had never seen him in action and she meant to seize the opportunity. She had only heard of his skill with the scalpel from fellow nurses at Hartlake in earlier years—and usually that had been much less praised than his dark good looks, she recalled dryly.

'Mr Armstrong!'

Blake checked with a hand on the swing door of the ward. 'Sister?' A glint of amusement mocked her formal tone as he ushered her before him into the corridor.

Jenefer stiffened. Perhaps she was too sensitive, but it seemed to her that he constantly sneered at her status. 'I'm sorry,' she said shortly, feeling that he expected an apology. 'I did explain that there are specially trained staff to take care of her, but she got so upset that I had to promise that I'd stay with her.'

'Anything to keep her blood pressure from soaring sky-high,' he agreed smoothly. 'Keep the patient happy at all costs. But we both know how busy you are, and she won't know if you're there or not once she's under and then you can return to the ward.'

It was so pointed that Jenefer instantly made up her mind to remain for the entire operation whether he liked it or not. 'Nurse Walsh is an excellent deputy,' she said firmly. 'And I like to keep my promises.' She deliberately stressed that point, but Blake appeared not to notice the acid allusion. She looked at him with a challenge in her hazel eyes. There was something that had to be said even if it provoked him to fresh anger. 'I'm worried, Blake. You've played down the dangers, but there's a real risk to Hilda in this operation, isn't there?'

'A calculated risk,' he drawled.

'And it's one that you don't really want to take, I suspect!'

His mouth hardened. 'I don't know what the devil you mean.'

'I think you're only operating to prove a point to Ryan Montague. I just hope that Hilda won't suffer as a result,' she said impulsively, trading on their past relationship, and saw the quick flare of anger in his dark eyes.

'Damn you, Jenefer! Whatever you may have heard, I'm still a competent surgeon and I don't make a practice of losing patients,' he said furiously, and strode away from her with the tautness of his tall figure shouting his annoyance that she had dared to question his professionalism.

Jenefer resisted a childish impulse to make a face at his retreating back and vented her discomfiture on a first-year nurse who was staring after the dark-haired surgeon in open admiration. 'Nothing to do, Nurse? I'm sure Nurse Bailey could use another pair of hands,' she snapped. 'There's no time to stand and stare on this ward!'

'No, Sister. I mean . . . yes, Sister. I mean—I *am* helping Nurse Bailey,' the girl stumbled, taken aback. 'She sent me to lay up a trolley . . .'

'Then I suggest that you get on with it!' And Jenefer bristled all the way back to her office and the unfinished paperwork, wishing she had never set eyes on Blake Armstrong and wishing even more fervently that he hadn't turned up at Pagett's to plague her.

CHAPTER SIX

JENEFER walked at the side of the trolley towards the lift that connected the wards with the top floor theatre unit, case notes in one hand and the other gripped with surprising strength by Hilda, who was apprehensive despite the pre-med injection.

'There's nothing to worry about,' she soothed for perhaps the twentieth time that morning, smiling at Hilda as the theatre porter skilfully manoeuvred the cumbersome trolley into the lift. 'You'll just go off to sleep and when you wake up it will all be over and you'll be back on the ward.'

There was no need to tell her that she would wake up on a different ward, she decided. For some time after surgery, Hilda wouldn't know or care where she was, and Jenefer intended to visit her on Jasper to see how she was getting on.

Escorting her patient from the lift to the ante-room that adjoined the operating-room of a theatre suite, she was instantly caught up in the unforgettable atmosphere of Theatres with its distinctive smells and sounds and deceptive absence of urgency. The corridors might be empty, but behind the scenes surgeons and anaesthetists and theatre staff were busily involved in curing disease and mending broken bodies.

Although she enjoyed her work as Sister Cresswell and was proud to be in charge of her own ward, Jenefer was briefly envious of the instant results and rewards of theatre work. Nursing, particularly on a

71

medical ward, could be a long-term business before a patient was well enough to be discharged, and sometimes there was little that could be done in cases of advanced illness or old age.

John Randall was waiting to receive the patient and a theatre nurse was preparing the injection that would put Hilda to sleep before she went into the operating-room. Another nurse made the routine check of the tag on Hilda's wrist to confirm that she was in fact the Hilda Maitland who was listed for neuro-surgery.

'Hallo, Hilda,' John said warmly with the informality that most patients appreciated. 'How do you feel? A little nervous? Nothing to worry about, you know. Just a little prick of a needle . . .' He turned to Jenefer. 'We don't see you here very often, Sister,' he said in smiling surprise.

'A visit to Theatre is a rare treat for me these days,' Jenefer agreed, rather wistfully.

'Miss it, do you? You were a very good theatre nurse.' John held aloft the syringe that the nurse handed to him, checking its contents. Then he inserted the fine point of the needle into a vein. Within seconds, Hilda's eyelids drooped and her mouth grew slack as the drug took effect. He checked pupils and pulse while the nurse removed the pillow so that Hilda lay flat on the trolley, ready to be wheeled into the operating theatre and prepped for surgery. 'I hope you're staying,' the anaesthetist added warmly. 'It should be an interesting morning.'

'I'm tempted,' Jenefer admitted. 'But I'm really not sure how he feels about it.' She nodded at the broad green-clad back of the surgeon as he stood at a basin in the scrub annexe, sluicing water over strong bare arms.

'Oh, I don't suppose he'll mind. You aren't likely to faint at his feet, are you?'

She laughed. 'He'd just step over me and carry on if I did,' she declared wryly.

Hearing the lilt of her laugh, Blake glanced over his shoulder with the crease of a frown between his eyes. Wounded by her insensitive jibe in the pub, angered by the doubt she had cast on his ethical integrity that morning, he felt that he didn't want her in the theatre when he needed all his concentration for the job in hand. She was a disturbing influence, having figured much too largely in his thoughts and dreams for years.

Shaking surplus water from hands and arms, he dried them on a sterile towel handed to him by a nurse. Another nurse helped him into his theatre gown and tied the strings with deft fingers. Blake thanked her with a glint of his attractive smile before he drew the mask up and over nose and mouth.

Thrusting his hands into skin-tight surgical gloves, he strode to the door of the ante-room, taking care not to cross the threshold in his rubber theatre boots, hands held high to avoid contact with an unsterile surface.

'How's the patient, John?'

'Nicely under. I'm just about to wheel her in . . .'

'Good.' Dark eyes above the mask skated over Jenefer. 'You ought to be wearing greens if we're to have the pleasure of your company, Sister.'

'I'll go and change.' Jenefer hurried away before he could rescind that brusque invitation, doubting that he would gain any pleasure from her presence and perversely determined to irritate him with it. If only because it would be interesting to compare his style and technique with the surgeons she had enjoyed assisting during her spell as a scrub nurse in Theatres.

She had liked the work for its drama and challenge as well as the informal atmosphere that was a welcome contrast to the tempo and tension of Theatres. She had been promised eventual promotion to Sister Theatres, but had decided that she preferred to be involved with patients as people rather than injured or diseased bodies in need of a surgeon's skill. She liked the caring and the continuity of ward work.

But she could understand the attraction of surgery for someone like Blake. A life lay in his hands, dependent on his skill and his judgment. A wrong move, a moment of doubt or inattention, could result in death or brain damage or permanent paralysis for his patient. In neuro-surgery he had chosen a delicate and difficult field, and Jenefer wondered if he enjoyed a sense of power, a godlike omnipotence, in the knowledge that he held the balance of a person's fate in his skilled hands.

But she couldn't doubt his dedication or his concern or his genuine desire to do his best to improve the quality of life for those who happened to need his expertise and his experience as well as his fearless grasp of new techniques.

As an observer, Jenefer didn't need to scrub up, but it was essential to exchange her crisp cap and dark blue dress for the anonymous green theatre frock and theatre slippers and mask and cover her shining hair with the regulation mob-cap.

She was anxious not to miss a moment, and she sped back to the operating theatre—to hesitate on the threshold at sight of a striking tableau. The theatre team was grouped about the table and some interested spectators stood in the background. Medical students and junior nurses attracted by the prospect of some exciting surgery had crowded into the viewing gallery. John Randall sat at the head of the table, perhaps the most important person in the room as he busied himself with a complexity of dials and valves, surrounded by monitors to check the level of consciousness, the rise or fall of blood pressure, the behaviour of heart and lungs.

Hilda was in position, covered with sterile drapes and with only a small portion of her head visible, newly shaved and painted bright yellow with acriflavine solution. The Theatre Sister stood with hand poised over the array of gleaming instruments while Blake listened patiently to the junior registrar who talked to him in low, urgent tones.

Sensing tension, Jenefer slipped quietly into place between Ryan and a theatre nurse, facing the surgeon and slightly to his left, giving her an excellent view of proceedings. She received the flicker of a glance from Blake before he returned his attention to his colleague.

Ryan looked down at her, the gleam of a smile in his eyes. 'Glad you could make it.'

'Not to be missed, you said. What's going on?' she asked curiously, low-voiced.

'Slight difference of opinion. Armstrong favours an unorthodox approach to the site of the problem. Barry thinks he should stick to the tried and tested. Armstrong says that he's familiar with a procedure that he's carried out a dozen times. Barry argues that it wil take longer and put Hilda at risk. Now you're up to date.'

Knowing Blake's forceful personality and compelling conviction that his skill and ability were second to none in his field, Jenefer had no doubt that he would win the argument.

Moments later, his deep voice cut across Barry Rowe's protest like a relentless scythe. 'We'll do it my way and I'll take full responsibility if anything goes wrong,' he said, and his tone left no one in any doubt that he had merely paid the young surgeon the compliment of listening when the decision was already made and final.

'Very well, sir . . .' Like it or not, Barry had to accept the situation. The tightness of his tone betrayed that he didn't like it at all, for until Blake's arrival he had been used to having things very much his own way in the Neuro-surgical Unit. It still rankled that he had been passed over for an older and more experienced man.

Blake was making himself unpopular, Jenefer felt. But dislike or disapproval seldom bothered him. He had too much confidence in himself, and his often unorthodox procedures had proved remarkably successful in the past, helping to build his reputation as one of Hartlake's top surgeons. However, here at Pagett's, he still had to prove himself to his new colleagues. Then he might be able to relax and make friends instead of alienating people with that autocratic attitude.

'Scalpel, please, Sister.'

Everyone tensed at the quiet request and Jenefer superstitiously crossed her fingers behind her back, willing things to go right. She was supposed to view every patient with a necessary detachment, but it was only human to pity the plight of one or to feel drawn to the personality of another, and she had a particularly soft spot for Hilda, admiring her courage and the fierce will to survive.

'He'll need to be just as good as he reckons he is to get our Hilda through this,' Ryan declared in a critical

undertone, and subsided as the surgeon silenced him
with a scowl.

Blake made the first incision with the precision and
economy of a first-class surgeon and then proceeded
to lay back the skin flap to expose the dura mater.
Jenefer had an excellent view, and she listened
spellbound as he guided team and spectators through
each stage of the following procedure, thrilling to his
superb mastery of his specialised field.

She envied the Theatre Sister who handed clamp or
forceps or retractor or swabbed where Blake
indicated. She would dearly love to be in Stella Stead's
shoes, she admitted wistfully, knowing that the
opportunity to assist a surgeon of Blake's calibre was
lost to her now that she had given up theatre work to
run her own ward. For the first time, she felt a twinge
of regret.

Once she would have glowed with pride in him and
basked in the reflected glory of being Blake
Armstrong's girl. Now, despite her feeling about the
man, she could still wholeheartedly admire the
surgeon, and she warmed to him as she watched those
sure, clever hands at their work.

He appeared to be confidence itself, but she noticed
how often he turned his head to have the glistening
beads of sweat wiped from his brow by the hovering
dirty nurse. She sensed the fierce intent of his
concentration as if the outcome of this operation was
of particular importance to him. As it was his first
opportunity to show off his special skills to a
respectful and admiring audience of Pagett's staff, he
was probably on his mettle, Jenefer decided.

Watching so closely, she saw the moment of
hesitation when his hands seemed unexpectedly
unsure of their next move. Her gaze moving

upwards, she saw the deep furrow of his brow and a
flicker of uncertainty in the dark eyes above the mask.
Her heart faltered with apprehension.

Blake met her eyes. For a moment he looked into
the gold-flecked depths, finding an unexpected but
welcome encouragement and belief in their glow.
Tension ebbed from his lean frame and he was once
more in control, nerveless hand striking to reveal the
suspicious bubble in the cerebral artery.

'Come closer, Montague,' he invited. 'I want you to
see this.'

Ryan edged forward to study the offending
aneurism. 'It appears to be saccular, as you
suspected,' he said wryly.

'Yes.' There was no trace of gloat in Blake's deep
voice. 'This is the real culprit, don't you think?' He
exposed a clump of fibrous tissue, minute but
dangerous. 'Attached to the trigeminal nerve and
lurking beneath the arterial wall.'

'Which explains why it didn't show on the scan.'

Blake nodded. 'Well, we didn't agree that surgery
was the answer in this case, but you were proved right
and if she recovers then she'll owe more to you than to
me,' he said, generously giving credit. 'I'll remove
this mass and send it to the Path Lab for analysis.
With luck, the damaged nerve will recover to some
extent. I'll ligate this aneurism too . . .' As he spoke,
outlining procedure, his hands were busy and necks
craned for a better view.

When he began the lengthy business of suturing
some time later, Jenefer slipped away, having been
out of the ward for longer than she had anticipated.

Her heart had steadied as soon as Blake resumed his
work, but she was sure that his confidence had briefly
and inexplicably deserted him at a critical stage

of surgery. She wondered if anyone else had noticed that tiny pause and his unease or if their one-time closeness had made her unusually sensitive to his feelings even at this late date.

How strangely he had looked at her, too! As if he drew strength and renewed confidence from her presence, she thought with a tremor along her spine. But perhaps it had all been imagination on her part.

Hot and sticky, head aching slightly from the heat and glare of overhead arc lights, hair and skin and clothes permeated by the sickly smells of ether and disinfectant, Jenefer thankfully stripped out of theatre greens and stepped under a refreshing cascade of hot water. She had forgotten the once-familiar ache of back and legs and feet from long standing in an operating theatre, she thought wryly.

But she wouldn't have missed that morning for anything.

Cresswell seemed another world. But, as she welcomed a patient admitted in her absence with acute chest pain, soothed a confused old lady who insisted that things were being taken from her locker by the nurses and the other patients, scolded a junior for gossiping with a houseman instead of supervising a frail patient in the bath and supplied tea and sympathy to a distressed relative, Jenefer felt that her ward was dominated just as Theatre had been by the forceful personality and powerful presence of a brilliant surgeon.

Later, coming out of a side ward after giving a morphine injection to a seriously ill patient, she discovered that Blake's imagined presence was in fact a reality.

Still wearing the V-necked tunic and thin cotton trousers of theatre greens, mask dangling by its strings, he stood outside the doors of the main ward, his handsome face wreathed in a smile as he talked to Ann Morley. With his crisp curls rumpled by the hasty removal of a theatre cap, he looked younger than his thirty-five years and much too attractive for any woman's peace of mind.

Jenefer froze in instant disapproval. Then, handing the kidney dish to a passing junior with instructions to dispose of its contents, she stalked towards the couple who seemed oblivious to everything and everyone but themselves.

They separated at her approach, nurse hastily backing through the swing doors into the ward and surgeon turning to Jenefer, his smile fading. 'There you are, Sister!'

The bland words implied that he had come to Cresswell for the sole purpose of speaking to her. Jenefer didn't believe it. 'Looking for me, Mr Armstrong?' she challenged crisply.

'You left before the end of the performance this morning. I hope it wasn't too much for you?'

Jenefer was surprised that an apparently preoccupied surgeon had noticed her absence from the theatre, but she stiffened with suspicion of that mockingly solicitous tone. 'I had to get back to the ward.'

'Of course—the indispensable Sister Gale,' he drawled.

Her mouth tightened. He might sneer, but she was proud of the navy dress and fluted cap and gleaming silver buckle of her Ward Sister's uniform. It was about the only reason she had to be grateful to him, she thought crossly. For if they *had* married then she would never have achieved that ambition.

'What can I do for you?' Her tone was cold.

'Perhaps you could spare me a few moments of your valuable time, Sister?'

Stiff-backed, Jenefer led the way into the office and put the broad expanse of the desk between them. She knew it was foolish, but she felt strangely threatened by his height and his powerful build and his maleness.

Blake studied her thoughtfully. 'I expect you've heard that Mrs Maitland survived my surgery.'

His sardonic tone irritated her. 'I don't doubt your surgical skill,' she retorted. 'Merely your integrity.'

Dark eyes blazed. Then the glow faded and he shrugged broad shoulders. He had no wish to quarrel with her. Too much pain had already been caused by hasty words and even hastier actions, in his opinion.

'Shall we try to avoid personalities and concentrate on doing our respective jobs as well as possible?' he suggested quietly.

It was well-deserved rebuke and Jenefer felt shrivelled. 'How *is* Hilda?' she asked.

'Poorly. But she'll do.' The words held the ring of confidence. Blake sat on the edge of the desk, swinging a long leg, regarding her as she shuffled papers and capped a pen and straightened an already-neat pile of forms, carefully not meeting his eyes. 'You take a special interest in her, apparently. Any particular reason?' He was aware that Penfold was her home town, and it had occurred to him that Hilda Maitland might be family or friend or one-time neighbour.

'Only that she's a fighter and I'd like to see her get well and go home if it's at all possible.' Jenefer looked up at him defensively. 'She's a lovely lady.'

A smile flickered across the impassively handsome face. She had always been defensive about her tendency to get emotionally involved with patients,

he recalled. Beneath all the starchy dignity, she was
still the girl he had known, the girl he still needed.

'She'll remain in Intensive Care for the time being
but, all being well, I'd like her to come back to
Cresswell,' he said abruptly.

Jenefer greeted the suggestion with mixed feelings.
It would be nice to have Hilda under her eye while she
convalesced, but she didn't welcome the attendant
necessity of seeing Blake on his frequent visits to the
ward to monitor his patient's progress. He disturbed
her too much.

She kept her hands busy to conceal their tendency
to tremble and carefully controlled her voice to
disguise its betraying quiver. For she didn't like what
Blake was doing to her as he sat on the corner of her
desk, overwhelming her with his very physical
presence, and she avoided his searching gaze so that
her own expressive eyes shouldn't reveal the amazing
turmoil of her emotions.

The heart could conquer a foolish sentimentality
about a past love. The mind could be resolute in
refusing to entertain the rush of memories. But it
seemed that weak and wilful flesh that had once
thrilled to a man's touch and kiss and ardent caress
could still crave and clamour for his embrace in spite
of every effort to suppress the wanton yearning.

Jenefer ached to reach out to Blake, to run her
fingers through the strong black curls and cradle his
handsome head in her hands, to trail her lips across
his lean cheek to the warmly sensual mouth and stir
his powerful body to a remembered passion with her
kiss.

They had once been lovers but could never be so
again, she told herself fiercely. For Blake was
married—and that discovery had put an end to

dreaming and crushed the last, still flickering embers of a flame that ought to have burned itself out with the years.

Love was dead—and longing must be kept well hidden beneath the stiff, starched bodice of the mature and sensible Ward Sister who had taken the place of a foolish first-year in love with a surgeon.

CHAPTER SEVEN

BLAKE put out a hand to remove the pencil that Jenefer was turning over and over between slender fingers as she gazed, not at him, but at some distant dream.

'Are you listening to me?' he demanded.

The snap of the words shocked her out of her reverie. 'Of course I am,' she said sharply, only vaguely aware that he had been outlining his reasons for wanting Hilda to be nursed on Cresswell.

'Then you agree?'

'In principle. But it isn't usual practice. Not here, anyway. In fact, arrangements have already been made for her transfer to Jasper when she leaves the ICU.'

'Then they must be unmade.'

It was so autocratic that Jenefer bridled. Star surgeons were often arrogant, but she felt that sweeping dismissal of her protest as a personal attack on her authority.

'It's most irregular for post-op patients to be nursed on a medical ward,' she said starchily.

Blake frowned. 'There isn't much that you can tell me about hospital procedure,' he reminded her dryly. 'I know it's irregular, but Mrs Maitland is in a highly anxious state and I think she'll benefit from being returned to surroundings and staff that are familiar to her.' He could have added that returning his patient to Cresswell would give him more opportunities to bridge the gulf that Jenefer seemed so determined to widen. 'It means weeks of special care, but no doubt you and your splendid team of nurses can cope with that.'

Sarcastic brute! Jenefer fumed. 'All my patients get special care,' she said snubbingly. 'I don't anticipate any problems in nursing Mrs Maitland.'

Blake rose abruptly. It had been a clumsy attempt at a compliment, but he seemed to have lost his ability to charm where Jenefer was concerned. 'Mrs Maitland isn't the problem, Sister. You are,' he said wearily, and strode from the room.

Jenefer was puzzled and vaguely hurt by the unmistakable note of disappointment in that deep voice. He couldn't possibly fault her work, she must be failing him on a personal level. But what had Blake expected from her? A warm, open-armed welcome, a readiness to forgive and forget, an instant return to loving? Was that why he hadn't mentioned the existence of a wife?

The man was an enigma, she decided crossly, and called to a nurse who was passing the open door. It was Ann Morley who hurried back to the office at the summons, and Jenefer wondered if the girl had been in pursuit of the departing surgeon.

'Mrs Maitland is coming back to Cresswell shortly,' she said crisply. 'Can you rescue her locker before it gets to Jasper Ward?'

'I think it's still around, Sister. We've been so busy . . . I'll check, shall I?'

'If you would.'

Ann lingered in spite of the briskly dismissive tone. 'How is she, Sister? Several patients have asked.'

Jenefer wondered dryly why the first-year hadn't asked the surgeon for news of his patient. She'd had

ample opportunity, chance or contrived. What *had*
they been talking about so earnestly in the corridor?
she wondered curiously.

'It was a long operation, but she seems to have come
through it all right. Mr Armstrong is quite optimistic,
I gather.' She liked to encourage a degree of
involvement between junior nurses and patients and
there was time to build up a rapport on a medical
ward. Most surgical wards had such a rapid turnover
that patients could still be strangers to the nurses
when they were due for discharge.

'He's very clever, isn't he?' Ann's tone was
admiring.

'He has that reputation,' Jenefer agreed coolly. She
didn't want to snub, but nor did she intend to discuss
Blake with the girl who had thrown herself at him as
soon as he arrived at Pagett's. Her reluctant liking for
Ann Morley was seriously undermined by a
resentment of Blake's obvious interest, and it was a
jealousy that she struggled to overcome. After all,
only his wife had any right to object.

She wondered if Ann knew that Blake was married.
With a mental shrug, she decided it was no part of her
duties as Sister Cresswell to safeguard the feelings or
the morals of the juniors—and the first-year was
certainly old enough to take care of herself!

'Everyone will be delighted to have Hilda back on
the ward,' Ann said warmly.

'It will mean a lot of extra work, of course.'

'No one will mind that, Sister!'

Jenefer couldn't help smiling. 'I'm sure *you* won't,
anyway.' Ann had proved an asset, after all, with her
enthusiasm and her willingness to tackle any chore,
however dirty or unpleasant. Jenefer saw herself at
eighteen, just as enthusiastic and eager to please

and anxious to do well. But it might be as well to repeat some advice that she had been given in her own first-year days. 'Don't let your feelings run away with you, will you, Nurse? It doesn't pay to get too fond of any of the patients. You must have been told in PTS that you need to acquire a second skin to survive as a nurse.'

Brenda Walsh overheard the light warning as she came into the room. 'Besides, it's a terrible waste when there are so many lonely and overworked doctors in need of a pretty nurse to hold their hand,' she added with an impish grin. 'Patients come and go, lass—and they're forgotten sooner than they like to think. Find yourself a nice young doctor to care about, that's my advice.' As Ann smiled and hurried away, she added dryly: 'I hear she's already chosen her man. The charmer from the NSU—Blake Armstrong. Some of these girls don't waste a minute, do they?'

'How do you find the time to listen to all the current gossip?' Jenefer marvelled dryly. 'This place is running alive with rumours and every one tells a different story!' She drew a form towards her and began to write out the drugs that she needed from Pharmacy from a list she had compiled earlier in the day. 'By this time next week that man's name will be linked with at least a dozen different nurses, I should imagine.'

'But yours won't be among them, I take it?' teased Brenda, her quick ear detecting a note of scornful dismissal behind the airy words.

Jenefer shrugged. 'Who knows? None of us seem to be safe from the gossips, and if there's nothing to talk about they aren't above inventing it.'

Brenda looked at the Ward Sister's bent head with a gleam of speculation in her narrowed eyes. Jenefer was just a little too indifferent to the attractive new surgeon from the NSU, she felt. 'People are saying he had to leave Hartlake in a hurry. Some scandal involving a patient, apparently. Unprofessional conduct.' The phrase rolled off her tongue with unmistakable relish.

The chestnut head reared in disbelief and immediate defence. 'They're saying *what*! Oh, what rubbish! Blake, unprofessional? They just don't know him if they think that!' The impulsive words spilled out before she could stop them.

Brenda eyed her curiously. 'But *you* do, obviously.'

Jenefer cursed the tongue that had run away with her and resigned herself to the inevitable. 'Knew him,' she amended, a little reluctantly. 'But it was a long time ago and it isn't worth resurrecting.'

'An old flame?' Brenda had scented romance and wasn't the type to be easily put off. 'Aren't you thrilled to bits to meet him again?'

'No, I'm not. And I'm not carrying a torch for him,' Jenefer asserted coldly. 'So don't make a big thing of it, Brenda. In any case, he's married.'

The staff nurse raised an eyebrow. 'Is he now? Well, he doesn't seem to be advertising the fact,' she said dryly. She closed the Kardex. 'I suppose you knew him when you were at Hartlake?'

'For a short time. But please don't spread it around—I don't want everyone talking about something that was over and done with years ago. He can't afford to have a lot of silly rumours affecting his career. Or his marriage.'

'Well, I won't breathe a word.'

Jenefer had no faith at all in the glib assurance as the staff nurse returned to the ward. In fact, she didn't doubt that such a juicy titbit of information would be passed on to a friend within minutes, complete with embroidery.

Perhaps it had been naïve to hope that she and Blake could keep a past romance from becoming common knowledge. Well, they had nothing to hide, she reminded herself. It was not a crime to change one's mind about marriage, after all.

Even if she had yet to forgive Blake for doing just that.

By ten o'clock that evening, Lucy's party was in full swing, many of her guests being doctors and nurses who knew how to enjoy themselves after a hard day on the wards.

Filling more rolls and sandwiches, cutting up quiches and gateaux and replenishing bowls of crisps and nuts and savouries, Jenefer was kept too busy in the kitchen to circulate. She had no time to miss Tom. In any case, he rather disapproved of Lucy and her exuberant lifestyle and let it show, and he could be a damper at parties, she had found. Jenefer might be a mature Ward Sister, but she could still enjoy a party even when it threatened to get out of hand. Lucy had a lot of friends who were encouraged to bring their friends along to her famous parties and as a result too many people were crushed into her small terraced house on occasions. Loud music and rather wild behaviour could attract some unsavoury gatecrashers too.

Jenefer hoped that the evening would be less lively than usual as she snatched an occasional sip of Martini and nibbled at a sandwich in between fending off the amorous attentions of Lucy's current boyfriend. Lucy was flirting with someone else and seemed to have forgotten that she was the hostess.

Like a good friend, Jenefer had stepped into the
breach, but she wasn't prepared to console Mark
Dawson for the temporary loss of Lucy's interest. She
pushed away his sneakily encircling arm, laughing at
his outrageous compliments, and kept a weather eye
out for Lucy, who was never generous with her men
even when she no longer wanted them. She had no
wish to quarrel over a man who didn't even appeal to
her!

People wandered in with empty glasses and stayed
to talk, voices raised to combat the deafening disco
music from the other room. The kitchen was hot and
airless and too crowded for comfort. Picking up a
plate of sandwiches, Jenefer escaped to the equally
crowded living-room and began to edge her way
through the crush of mostly unknown revellers.

Ann Morley was there, flamboyantly attractive in a
silk trouser suit, vivid splashes of scarlet and green
and orange against a cream background. Jenefer felt
almost dowdy by comparison in her quietly elegant
black dress with its slash of silver brocade across skirt
and bodice, matching the high-heeled silver sandals
and dangling silver ear-rings. On impulse, she had
slipped on the silver bracelet that had lain too long in
its hiding-place, telling herself that it was silly not to
wear it sometimes.

She paused to speak to Ann. 'Hallo. Having a good
time?' She looked round for Ryan, who had spoken of
steering the first-year in the direction of Lucy's party.
She couldn't see him anywhere in the room.

'It's great, isn't it?' Ann enthused.

'Have a sandwich . . .'

'Thanks.' She helped herself with a sparkle of her
friendly smile. 'There's nothing like nursing to
improve a girl's appetite. I shall probably put on

pounds!'

'Most of us do,' Jenefer smiled, secure in her own sylph-like slenderness that never altered by so much as an ounce.

'Blake's here somewhere—circulating. Have you seen him yet?'

The easy manner and the confident use of the surgeon's first name with its implications of a close friendship jarred on Jenefer. 'I hope he's brought his wife with him,' she said sweetly.

Ann stared. 'His wife . . .?' Her eyes darkened and narrowed. 'Do you mean *Cheryl*?'

Jenefer shrugged. 'If that's her name.'

'But she *died*!'

There was so much noise in the room that Jenefer wasn't sure that she had heard correctly. After all, it was so *unlikely*. Wasn't it?

'Sorry . . .? I thought you said . . .'

'Last year—leukaemia. I thought you knew.'

Jenefer was too shocked to wonder at Ann's strangely wooden expression or the machine-gun delivery of the words. 'No, I didn't know. How dreadful!' she said blankly, stunned. Suddenly seeing Blake by the open french window that gave access to a long, overgrown garden, she impulsively thrust the plate of sandwiches at Ann. 'Here, hand these round for me, will you? I must speak to Blake . . .'

She pushed and shoved without apology to reach him, sick at heart when she thought of the way she had jibed at him. It was no excuse that she hadn't known about his marriage or its tragic end. Besides, Blake might not realise that fact. She had been spiteful and he might think she had meant to hurt, seeking a petty revenge for the pain and disappointment he had caused her. She must rid his mind of that suspicion at the very least!

She clutched at his sleeve. 'Blake!'

He turned to look at her, impassive, dark eyes inscrutable. 'I heard you were here.'

Well, he hadn't come looking for her to say hello—and how could she blame him? 'About the other night,' Jenefer began awkwardly. 'I'm sorry—I didn't know . . .'

There was no need for Blake to ask what she had learned. Her stricken face said it all. But her previous lack of knowledge implied an indifference that was even more hurtful to him than the words she had thrown at him in the pub. He arched a dark eyebrow. 'Would it have made a difference?'

'If I'd known? Of course! You can't think that I'd *want* to hurt you, surely!' She was dismayed by the doubt and distrust she sensed in his attitude.

'Your past record isn't in your favour,' Blake said levelly.

'*My* past record . . .?'

'You said a lot of things without caring if they hurt. Or if they were true.'

'So did you!' Jenefer flared hotly. Then, with an effort, she caught at the tail of her temper. 'Look, there's no point in arguing about ancient history, Blake. I *am* sorry and I *didn't* know about your wife—truly!'

'Then your usual informants let you down badly, didn't they?' he drawled.

Jenefer bit her lip. Privately she agreed, although she was too loyal to her Hartlake friends to say so. But it was puzzling that not one of them had told her about Blake's marriage—or his wife's death.

'They must have known, I suppose?' she ventured doubtfully.

'Everyone knew. Everyone was very kind.'

It was so brusque that Jenefer immediately understood just why he had given up a consultancy that could no longer have meant very much to him for a job at Pagett's where no one knew him. He must have been desperate to get away from Hartlake and well-meaning friends and painful reminders of the wife he had loved and lost with such terrible finality.

Her heart went out to him on a surge of compassion. It must have been dreadful for Blake to know that there was nothing that even a brilliant surgeon could do for a dying wife.

'You've been through a bad time,' she said quietly. 'You can't want to talk about it now, I know. But any time you need a friend—well, you know where to find me, Blake.'

'Thanks.' He had learned to mistrust some manifestations of sympathy, particularly from women who hoped to take Cheryl's place in his life. He didn't really doubt Jenefer's sincerity, but he resented the implication that she would open her arms to him out of pity.

As Blake turned away on the curt word. Jenefer felt that she wasn't forgiven—or needed, as friend or anything else. She swallowed hurt. For she ached to offer him comfort and consolation.

Last year, Ann had said, knowing so much more than she did that Blake must have confided in the first-year. Still recent enough to be painful and perhaps too recent for him to find consolation with any woman, least of all herself. But the knife twisted in an old wound as Jenefer watched him stroll towards Ann with a warm smile and saw the girl's hand outstretched in eager welcome.

She slipped out to the garden, glad of the cool

night air on her face, glad of a respite from the loud
music and incessant chatter and the need to keep a
smile pinned to her lips. She wandered towards the
dark of the distant boundary and retreated hastily as
she disturbed an entwined couple in the shadows.
Pausing in the shelter of an enormous rhododendron
bush that had been allowed to grow wild, she crossed
her arms across her breasts in the effort to ease a dull
ache.

It was dreadful to be jealous of a dead girl who had
known such shortlived happiness with the man she
loved. But her heart wrenched painfully at a vision of
Blake and his bride, standing at the altar and
exchanging age-old vows.

She no longer loved Blake. But some of the hurt of
loving and losing him still lingered, and it quickened
anew as she huddled beneath the damp arch of bush
away from the lights and noise and demands of Lucy's
party. For *she* should have stood with Blake at the
altar and heard his deep voice murmur '*I will*' and
seen the light of love in his dark eyes and felt that she
had reached the pinnacle of happiness as his bride.

She stood with her back to the house and its noisy
revellers, face lifted to the sky with its panoply of
bright stars. Once Blake had seemed just as distant,
just as unattainable—a star surgeon who would never
have time to notice a mere junior nurse. But he had
smiled, spoken, whisked her heart into his keeping
with his charm and his kiss, and for a short time she
had dared to dream.

Jenefer felt a welling sadness for all that she and
Blake might have shared if only he had loved her
enough, and a lone tear slid gently down her cheek. It
might have hurt less then and now if she had ever
understood just why and how she had failed a man

she loved so much, she thought bleakly.

Strong arms caught and held her, so tightly that she gasped. 'Got you!' Mark Dawson aimed a drunken kiss that missed her mouth and skated across her ear.

Startled and furious, Jenefer twisted in his arms and thrust both hands between herself and his hard, pushing body. 'Let me go, you idiot! You'll upset Lucy!' she warned, managing a light laugh.

'*She* doesn't care. *I* don't care. Don't want Lucy. Want you, you lovely creature . . .' He clamped his mouth fiercely over her lips.

She stood like stone as she suffered that hot, wet kiss, marble lips firmly closed against the offensive probe of his tongue, slender body stiff with outrage. Over Mark's shoulder she saw Blake, framed in the open doorway, the light behind him so that she couldn't make out the expression on his shadowed face. But his height and the shape of his handsome head and his once-familiar stance were unmistakable. So was the scorn in his deliberately raised voice as he spoke to the girl at his side.

'These parties are all the same—just an excuse for drunks and silly women to make fools of themselves. Not my scene. Nor yours, I imagine, Ann? Time to go before things get really sordid, don't you think?'

Jenefer wrenched herself out of Mark's hateful embrace, resisting the impulse to hit him hard, for he was too drunk to know what he said or did. 'Leave me alone!' she snapped, and headed for the house.

Mark lurched in her wake. 'Whassamarrer, darling? Not in the mood? I'll soon alter that if you only give me half a . . .' he hiccuped, giggled. 'Half a chance!'

Jenefer evaded greedy hands that reached for her. 'Oh, do grow up!' she exclaimed. Losing all patience, she shoved him away with such force that he lost his drunken balance.

He fell awkwardly, catching the side of his head on a stone urn that was half hidden by the long, unkempt grass of a one-time lawn. He sat up, rubbing his temple with a bewildered, slightly reproachful look in his eyes, and then he uttered an odd little sound, half sigh, half groan, and slumped.

'Blake! There's something wrong here!'

About to turn away with a curl to his lip, the surgeon checked at that urgent appeal. 'Your boyfriend's passed out, that's all,' he said curtly. But he left Ann's side to stride across the grass towards Jenefer.

Kneeling beside her, he was so close that the tang of after-shave and his body warmth evoked a rush of memories and an unexpected tingle of response to his maleness. His shoulder grazed her cheek as he leaned across her to find the pulse in Mark's neck, and her heart lurched as she stared at the strongly handsome profile of the man she had once loved so much.

'Out like a light,' he confirmed impatiently. 'He won't come to much harm if he's left out here to sleep it off!'

Jenefer looked at him, doubtful. 'He *is* very drunk, but . . .' Meeting his eyes, knowing the sudden melt of her flesh, she was momentarily thrown, forgetting Mark, forgetting their surroundings, forgetting everything but Blake's nearness and dearness and discovering in that split second that nothing had changed. She still *cared.* Shock sent thoughts reeling and senses skittering and the blood draining from her face. 'He—I . . . I think he hit his head,' she blurted as he frowned, waiting for her to continue. 'Somewhere here . . .' As her hand reached out to touch Mark's temple, the silver bracelet spilled across her wrist to gleam in a shaft of light from the house behind them.

CHAPTER EIGHT

BLAKE tensed, staring at the bracelet that he instantly recognised as his birthday gift to her of six years earlier. He wondered why she had kept it—and why she had worn it that evening. To remind herself of all that happened between them, perhaps—and to warn herself not to let it happen again, he thought wryly.

It had hurt to see her in another man's arms. He hadn't expected to find that there were no men in her life, of course. She was much too attractive. But men like this one—drunk, uncouth, noisy, pawing her like an animal! What had happened to the lovely girl who had been so sensitive, so fastidious, so hard to get in those days at Hartlake?

With an effort, he brought his mind back to the present and the prone man. 'He could be concussed . . .' He lifted an eyelid and frowned. 'Perhaps we ought to get him into the house so I can have a proper look at him,' he said abruptly, getting to his feet and brushing trampled grass from his trouser knees.

As if on cue, Ann hurried out of the house, followed by two men she had recruited to help. 'Here comes the Cavalry!' she fluted lightly.

'Good girl! Just what we need!' Blake's welcoming smile was warm with approval.

Pain stabbed Jenefer as she realised their closeness, their affection for each other. No wonder there was no real place for her in Blake's life these days, she thought heavily. His overture of friendship had been just that and no more. Well, what had she expected after six years?

She scrambled to her feet as the burlier of the two men slid his hands beneath Mark's shoulders and his friend took hold of Mark's ankles. Between them, they carried the unconscious man into the house and laid him on a hastily vacated sofa.

People crowded round curiously.

'Is he dead? He's an awful colour . . .'

'Dead drunk!'

'Seriously, darling, he does look ill!'

'Was it a fight? Does Lucy know?'

'Where *is* Lucy?'

'Best not to ask, old man!'

'Is there a doctor in the house?' The dry query raised a laugh, for the house was bursting at the seams with medical men.

'Is there a *sober* doctor in the house?' someone capped, to more laughter.

Ignoring the babble of voices and the crowd around him, Blake carried out a brief but comprehensive examination. He sought and found Jenefer's anxious eyes as she hovered in the background. 'You say he hit his head?'

'I'm sure he did. On that stone thing in the garden—a pineapple or whatever it is!'

Blake nodded. 'Well, he isn't showing any sign of coming round yet. It's probably just a mild concussion, but we won't take any chances.' He looked up at Ann as she leaned over the back of the sofa, eager to help. 'Call an ambulance, will you?'

She hurried away to telephone. Jenefer went in search of Lucy and found her sitting on the kitchen floor with her new admirer, sharing a bottle of vodka between them. More drunk than sober, she seemed to be unaware of the commotion in the living-room, and it took some time to convince her that there was any real cause to be concerned about Mark. The arrival of the summoned ambulance was more effective than anything that Jenefer could say or do.

Jenefer managed to keep the tail-light of the ambulance in view as she ferried a distraught Lucy across town to the hospital. She did her best to stay calm and concentrate on her driving in spite of her own desperate anxiety about Mark.

She knew that Blake was worried, although he had said very little to her. He had opted to travel in the ambulance to keep Mark under continuous observation, leaving Ann Morley to make her own way home as the party fizzled out—and Jenefer couldn't feel even the slightest prick of her conscience that she hadn't offered the girl a lift into town at least. Her hands were full with Lucy, whose sense of guilt led her to blame everyone but herself for what had happened—and particularly Jenefer.

'I don't understand what you and Mark were *doing* out in the garden, anyway,' Lucy said suspiciously, her speech slightly slurred.

Jenefer sighed as she sensed the wave of hostility behind the words. 'Not what you think,' she said firmly. But she knew that she was wasting her words. Lucy was in no mood to believe anything but the worst of her, she thought ruefully.

'I thought I could trust you! You're supposed to be a friend!' It was accusing, bitter.

'I went out for some air, and Mark followed me. He'd had too much to drink and he made a pass. That kind of thing happens at parties, Lucy. It doesn't mean a thing,' Jenefer soothed.

'You must have led him on! I expect you've been

fancying him for ages!'

Jenefer gave up. There was no point in denying such an absurd accusation or trying to defend herself while Lucy was in her present fuddled state of mind. In the light of a new day, she would know how silly it had been to think ill of a very good friend and hasten to apologise.

She was probably not the only one to believe that she and Mark had been in the shadowed garden to exchange a few kisses behind Lucy's back, she thought wryly. Certainly Blake had seen them together and leapt to all the wrong conclusions.

But she was trying not to think about Blake. There would be plenty of time to dwell on that sudden resurgence of feeling and all its implications when she knew that Mark was going to be all right . . .

Jenefer brought the Fiat to a halt in the hospital car park with a slight squeal of brakes. The ambulance had drawn up outside the Accident and Emergency Department. Tumbling from the car, Lucy ran to watch as Mark was brought out on a stretcher trolley and then wheeled into the building.

Jenefer arrived just as Blake stepped down from the ambulance. 'How is he, Blake?' she ventured anxiously.

The surgeon brushed past her, concerned for the unconscious man and intent on passing on his findings to the Casualty Officer, who had been alerted by radio. 'No change,' he said brusquely.

The hard light in those dark eyes dismayed her. Did he share Lucy's suspicion that she had made a deliberate play for Mark and despise her for it?

The Casualty Officer was an old friend who listened patiently to Lucy's garbled account of events and then turned to Jenefer for a more lucid explanation.

'I don't suppose there's much wrong with him,' he said reassuringly. 'He's had worse knocks on the rugger field and been back on his feet in a few days. Get yourself some coffee from the machine while I run the rule over him.'

The two girls waited in an agony of anxiety while he joined the neuro-surgeon in the cubicle where Mark had been taken for examination. It seemed an age before he reappeared and crossed to the bench where they sat in their party frocks, in vivid contrast to the stark simplicity of uniformed nurses and white-coated doctors.

'Concussion,' Mike Lloyd confirmed. 'We can't be sure yet how bad it is, but there are some disturbing signs. So we'll do some X-rays and admit him for observation.'

Lucy burst into tears.

Comforting her friend, Jenefer lost sight of Blake, who had come out of the cubicle and walked away while Mike was talking. There was no reason for him to wait around now that he had handed over responsibility for Mark to a colleague, of course. But she was foolishly hurt that he hadn't bothered to ask how she felt or to wish her goodnight before he left.

Perhaps he had been in a hurry to get back to Ann Morley. Jenefer wondered bleakly if the surgeon meant to spend what was left of the night in the first-year's arms.

Lucy refused to go home until Mark had been X-rayed and admitted to the Intensive Care Unit and she had been allowed a few minutes with her unconscious boyfriend. Waiting in the corridor for her friend Jenefer tried not to dwell on the implications of that prolonged spell of unconsciousness. Coma, for instance. One of the drawbacks to being a nurse was knowing too much about all the things that could go wrong, she thought wryly.

She glanced up as Mike came out of a nearby clinical room, followed by Blake. She had been so sure that the surgeon had left much earlier that surprise showed in her lovely face.

The Casualty Officer paused, smiling. 'Still here, Jenefer? There's nothing you can do, you know. Go home and get some sleep,' he suggested kindly.

'I'm waiting for Lucy. She insisted on seeing Mark.' Jenefer indicated the large envelope that he carried, knowing it contained X-rays. 'Bad news?'

'It isn't good,' Blake said bluntly. 'There's some indication of subdural haemorrhage. If he doesn't come round soon then we must do a brain scan and it may be necessary to operate.'

Jenefer had been trained to hide her feelings, but she had to swallow hard to cope with the blow of the words and the rebuke in his deep voice. A smile, a friendly word, would have helped a lot, but Blake was behaving as if they were total strangers.

Lucy came out of Mark's room at that moment, still tearful. She shot a baleful glance at Jenefer and marched off down the corridor without a word.

Jenefer sighed. 'I'd better get her home.'

Mike patted her shoulder, a little awkwardly. 'She'll feel better about things in the morning,' he comforted. Lucy had given her version of events to anyone who would listen, painting Jenefer black in the process. The story of the Ward Sister and the drunken doctor would be all over Pagett's within twenty-four hours, and he sympathised with Jenefer's situation.

Mike meant well, but she wished that *someone*

would give her the benefit of the doubt. It wasn't entirely her fault that Mark was lying in a hospital bed with concussion! But it seemed that everyone thought she was to blame. Including Blake—and his opinion seemed to count for more than she cared to admit.

In fact, Blake didn't know what to believe, swayed by disappointment and Lucy's flow of invective, reluctant to accept that Jenefer could have changed so much in six years. He wasn't a sentimental man, but he had clung to the memory of her as someone essentially good and straight and fine, someone who was incapable of cheating or cheap behaviour, and it was hard to see that image shattered before his eyes.

But if it was true that she had been encouraging Dawson to cheat on his girlfriend why had she thrust the man away so fiercely that he fell, knocking himself out on a garden ornament? Had it been a sudden revulsion of feeling, disgust with herself as well as the drunken lout who had smothered her with kisses and roamed all over her slight body with impertinent hands? Or had she merely become aware that they were in full view of anyone standing at the open french windows and been overcome with embarrassment?

He caught up with Jenefer as she left the hospital to follow her friend, who was rapidly making her way towards the car park. 'Can you give me a lift to Lucy's place? I need to pick up my car.' He had meant to be friendly, to smile, but both tone and smile were frozen by the ice in her expression as she turned.

'Of course.' He was so cold, so aloof, so unfriendly that Jenefer couldn't even muster a smile. She walked silently at his side, feeling that she had been tried and found guilty, trying to convince herself that it didn't matter *what* Blake thought. Or felt.

Her chilly silence, her stiff attitude, was yet another rebuff, Blake decided . . . more proof that she had lost all interest. What a fool he was to have imagined that she might be glad to see him again, might still care something for him, might welcome him with open arms and a generous heart!

Lucy waited beside the locked Fiat, tapping an impatient foot, not so outraged by Jenefer's behaviour that she was prepared to make her own way across town at that hour. Still without speaking, she got into the back of the car. She leaned forward to smile an invitation at the surgeon and, after a moment's hesitation, Blake swung his powerful frame on to the seat at her side.

Perhaps it wasn't a deliberate snub, but it certainly felt like it to Jenefer. She slid behind the wheel and turned the ignition key, a mix of hurt and indignation welling in her breast.

It seemed a long drive through deserted streets, past shuttered shops and silent houses. Glancing in the rear mirror, Jenefer saw that Blake had an arm about Lucy as he talked to her in low, reassuring tones. She couldn't hear what he said, but Lucy responded by pouring out all her fears and her feelings about Mark, together with a spiteful indictment of Jenefer's popularity and principles.

Jenefer was appalled as she heard herself described as a predatory and promiscuous female who couldn't keep her hands off any man, even when he belonged to her best friend.

She could make allowance for the fact that Lucy was naturally upset and anxious as well as muddled by too much alcohol, but it was a dreadful shock to learn that so much resentment and jealousy lurked behind a façade of friendship.

In vino veritas. Except that nothing Lucy had said about her behaviour or her morals was true, she thought dispiritedly, gripping the wheel so tightly as she drove in hurt, proud silence that her hands ached by the time they reached Lucy's house on the other side of Penfold. But that ache was nothing to the pain in her heart as she realised that Blake had probably believed every word of the torrent that Lucy had poured into his ear during the journey.

He hadn't said a single word in her defence, she thought unhappily. Well, it was a long time since he had known her well enough to believe in her integrity. He had changed so much in the intervening years. Perhaps he felt that she had too . . .

As she clambered out of the car and looked at the house with its still-blazing lights and the sound of music pouring out into the night from the hi-fi that no one had thought to turn off, Lucy burst into fresh tears.

In spite of her hurt and her disappointment in someone who had been a friend since their training days, Jenefer couldn't ignore Lucy's distress. Putting an arm around her, she steered her down the path and through the open front door, expecting Blake to walk away to his own car, parked some distance down the road, and drive off into the night.

Instead, he followed them into the house without hesitation. While Jenefer made tea and persuaded Lucy to drink it and to swallow some aspirin, he cleared some of the debris of the party, dumping bottles and half-eaten food, emptying ash-trays and rinsing glasses like an old hand at the business of clearing up after a riotous evening.

He had probably been a marvellous husband, Jenefer thought bleakly—and then hastily skated off the thin ice of envy. *She* was alive and well and reasonably content with her lot. Cheryl Armstrong had died much too young—and known that she was dying, no doubt. Jenefer didn't think that *she* could be capable of courage in such circumstances. But perhaps Blake had been a tower of strength to the wife he loved.

Coming down after she had helped Lucy to undress and get into bed, she found him in the living-room, surveying a much improved scene, having turned off the hi-fi and most of the lights and secured the French doors that had been left open as an invitation to intruders.

She smiled at him gratefully. 'Thanks very much, Blake. You've been an enormous help. The place was a mess!'

Everyone else had abandoned the party without a thought for the chaos they left behind. Jenefer went round the room, plumping cushions, picking items of crushed food from the carpet, discovering a handbag and a man's shoe behind the sofa, making work to take her mind off Blake's tall and troublesome presence. She sensed his dark eyes following her every move, intent and searching and so cold that a little shiver trickled down her spine.

Blake stood in the middle of the room with hands rammed into his pockets to prevent them from reaching out for the girl in her striking black and silver dress. Silver ear-rings swung back and forth against her slim neck as she bent and straightened in the process of tidying the room. The silver bracelet gleamed as it slid up and down her slender wrist, burning a brand of memory into his mind and heart.

Desire stirred along with memories evoked by the perfume she still favoured, the gleam of her chestnut curls in the warm light, the glimpse of an enticing curve of her breast as the bodice of her dress gaped when she stooped to pick something from the carpet. His mouth dried and his heart began to thud as the blood coursed strongly along his veins.

He was flesh and blood like any other man, and he couldn't mourn Cheryl for ever—and why had he come to Penfold if not to find Jenefer and urge her into his arms and wrap her around with the love that had never really left him?

He took a step towards her.

Jenefer glanced at him over her shoulder. 'I'll leave the rest till morning . . .' Her voice trailed off as she saw the burning in his eyes. Her heart soared into her throat. Then she scolded herself for allowing her imagination to run away with her. The days when Blake had looked at her with love and longing were long gone and she mustn't indulge in wishful thinking! 'I expect you want to get home, Blake,' she said brightly. 'It's very late.'

'Are you staying?'

'I think I should. I can't abandon Lucy when she's in such a state.' She smiled wryly. 'Besides, I can't trust her not to start drinking again as soon as my back is turned!'

Blake regarded her thoughtfully. 'Is she always so emotional?'

'Only when she's feeling the effects of too much vodka!' Recalling Lucy's flirtatious behaviour that evening and how little she had apparently cared if it upset Mark, she added acidly: 'I had no idea that Mark mattered so much to her!'

'Well, that's a point in your favour, I suppose,' he observed.

Jenefer was stung by the sardonic tone. 'I know

what you thought you saw, but you were mistaken, Blake! And I hope you know me better than to believe all the rubbish that Lucy was spouting in the car!'

He shrugged. 'It seems to me that I don't know you at all these days.' His hand shot out to capture her wrist in a powerful clasp. 'For instance, the girl I used to know would never have flaunted this in my face!' he said tautly.

Colour flooded into her face, more from the tingling shock of his touch than from embarrassment, although she wouldn't have worn the bracelet if she had known that they would meet that evening.

'It goes with this dress,' she said lamely.

Blake arched a sceptical eyebrow. 'I'm not stupid, Jenefer,' he retorted impatiently. 'You wore it to remind me that we used to be lovers. *Didn't you?*'

'I didn't even know that you were coming to the party! You really are the most conceited . . . *oh*!' Her breath fled on a gasp of surprise as he kissed her, his warm mouth covering her own and insisting on a response to its magic.

Jenefer closed her eyes, melting, as his arms went round her. It was a dream, just like so many that she had known through the years. Soon she would wake, bereft and lonely, tasting salt on her lips from the tears that had flowed as she slept. But this time it was an incredibly vivid dream.

The crispness of his thick curls beneath her fingers as she put her arms round his neck and yielded her body to his embrace. The warm skin of his neck and face, the slight roughness of a strong beard, the hint of after-shave and cologne mingling with male sweat. The powerful ripple of the muscles in his back and shoulders and chest. The lean line of hip and thigh and leg pressing against her and the throbbing heat in him as he held and kissed her and urged her down to the cushions of the sofa. Too vivid, setting her on fire, compelling the rush of desire that flooded all her senses and swept away resistance.

She clung to the dream, surrendering to its sweet sensuality, giving him kiss for kiss as his arms enclosed her and his clever hands moved over her in familiar urgency. His kiss became deeper, demanding, his caress more intimate as his fingers stole beneath the flimsy material draped over her breasts.

Jenefer trembled at his touch, so tender, so sure, so long desired, and her body flamed as his lips followed the exploring hand. Wave upon wave of longing swept through her as she held his head to her breast and stroked the thick crop of black curls. She wanted him desperately. Her heart had ached for him and her body had craved for him for so long. It seemed beyond belief that he was here, in her arms, murmuring her name as if it was an endearment, his powerful body shuddering with the passion that had conquered her in the past.

But when she woke from this wonderful dream—what then? Would Blake walk away again, no more in love with her than he had ever been? It seemed to Jenefer that the bracelet had reminded him of past loving and triggered present desire that would be soon forgotten. No doubt he believed that what she had once given so gladly was not likely to be denied to him now.

Well, he was mistaken, she determined, finding that pride was even more powerful than the tug of newly awakened desire. She *wouldn't* love him again! She *wouldn't* give again with the overwhelming eagerness of an eighteen-year-old who thought she had woven an indestructible spell about a star surgeon simply because she loved him with all her heart.

CHAPTER NINE

JENEFER twined her fingers in his hair and tugged. Blake raised his head. 'I don't know what you hoped for, but it isn't working,' she said firmly.

'Well, it was worth a try,' he countered lightly, smiling into hazel eyes that looked back at him so coldly that his heart failed him.

He had sensed her change of mood in the sudden tensing of her slender body, so nearly his own again, so abruptly denied to him. He was filled with a disappointment more acute than desire.

'And you thought I'd be easy!' Jenefer thrust him from her in sudden anger.

'No. I thought you might remember—the way I do,' he said quietly. He sat up and straightened his tie, refusing to despair. In her own time, Jenefer would come to him. He was sure of it. He had rushed his fences, that was all. She wasn't yet ready to rediscover the love for him that he believed to be deeply buried but far from dead.

'I don't think there's anything to be gained from trying to recapture the past.' Jenefer's heart trembled, but she refused to be swayed by his charm, his smoothly persuasive tongue. 'I think you'd better go, Blake.'

Blake got to his feet, so cool and so outwardly controlled that she could have no suspicion of the dismay that warred with the raging torment of disappointed desire within him. He stooped to pick up the bracelet that had fallen to the floor, one of its delicate links broken. He laid it carefully on the palm of his hand and looked down at it for a moment, expressionless, before holding it out to her. 'I'm sorry . . .'

She didn't know if he referred to the broken trinket or his failure to rekindle the brief enchantment of the past.

'It isn't important,' she said stiffly, the lie concealing her hurt that the bracelet had been a casualty of that passionate and pointless encounter. It was her own fault. Something so fragile and so precious to her should have been kept safe along with her heart and her pride, she thought wryly. Instead, she feared she had worn them all on her sleeve.

Officially off duty, Jenefer was able to spend much of the following day in ICU, talking to the staff and helping with their demanding routines in between sitting for long spells beside Mark's bed and watching for some sign of returning consciousness.

He had slipped into coma during the night, dread come true. That blow on the temple had done serious damage, and Jenefer couldn't help feeling that she was responsible. An unfortunate accident, her friends insisted, but she knew better. She had vented an angry jealousy of Blake's attachment to Ann Morley on poor Mark and he was seriously ill as a result.

She caught a glimpse of Blake as he strode into the unit and then joined Mike Lloyd in the office to discuss the results of the brain scan that had been carried out that morning.

She was checking the saline drip, studying the pale, remote face and half expecting Mark to draw his last breath at any moment, when the surgeon came up behind her and reached for the chart.

'I thought you were off duty this weekend,' he said

brusquely.

She was surprised that he was so well informed. 'I couldn't relax, and the unit can always use an extra pair of hands.' She turned to look at him, wary. 'It's bad news, isn't it?'

'I'm afraid it is. A ruptured blood vessel is leaking into the subdural cavity. I'm operating right away.'

Jenefer caught her breath. 'It's that urgent?'

'Don't look so anxious, Jenefer. He'll be all right,' Blake said reassuringly. But there was always an element of risk and he was rather more anxious than he was admitting. Least of all to Jenefer, who had good reason to dread the worst.

'Can I take that as a promise?' she asked, trying to smile.

Blake frowned. 'I'm not God.'

'Next best thing, perhaps?'

'Don't put too much trust in me,' he warned.

'I've lost a patient or two in my time.'

'Recently?' she suggested impulsively.

He arched an eyebrow. 'What makes you ask?'

'I just wondered . . .' Jenefer hesitated. With a hand on his arm, she drew him further from the bed. No one really knew what coma patients could hear or sense and she didn't want any of their exchange to reach Mark. 'The other day, when you were operating on Hilda Maitland, I had the strangest feeling—oh, I don't know—that you were remembering an occasion when a patient *didn't* survive your surgery.'

Blake recalled the moment. In the middle of delicate micro-surgery, his confidence had abruptly deserted him. Meeting Jenefer's eyes across the operating table, he had seen such a blaze of admiration in their depths that his nerve had instantly steadied. He had been warmed and encouraged by her obvious faith in his surgical ability, whatever she felt about him as a man.

'You're very perceptive,' he said quietly.

'Then I'm right?' Jenefer was pleased but disturbed by the proof of a lingering affinity between them.

'As it happens.'

'Tell me . . .?' It was low, too tentative to be pressing.

'Not much to tell.' But, looking down at her lovely face with its warm expression of interest and concern, Blake was prompted to confide in her. 'Cheryl had just died and I ignored some good advice and went on working when I should have taken a break. I was tired and I had a lot on my mind, and that led to an error of judgment.'

'And the patient died,' she sympathised.

'It was very much a last-ditch attempt to save that particular man, in any case. He would have died without surgery. His relatives felt that he died because of it and insisted on an inquiry. I'd tried a new procedure and that might have gone against me. Fortunately, the Board cleared me of blame. By which time I'd resigned.'

'Letting someone else take the consultancy that you'd worked for all those years!'

'That followed, of course. But, as I told you, I'd already decided that I didn't want it. Hartlake had been a terrific help to my career, but it played havoc with my personal life. Perhaps I was *too* ambitious . . .' He broke off with a shrug of broad shoulders. 'I took a six-month sabbatical and then this job came along. Mrs Maitland was a similar case and I guess I was nervous. I suppose it showed,' he added with a wry smile.

'Only to me,' Jenefer assured him swiftly.

Blake looked down at her. 'She's doing very well,' he sidetracked. 'I think she'll be one of my successes.'

'I'm sure of it,' she said warmly.

Blake wondered why she was being so sweet, so supportive, so friendly. Last night she had thrust him out of Lucy's house as if she wanted to thrust him out of her life too!

'I don't know if I can do as well by Dawson,' he warned abruptly.

'I know you'll do your absolute best,' Jenefer told him, quietly confident.

He looked away from the shining eyes that riveted his heart. 'I can't perform miracles, however,' he reminded her lightly. He wished he could. For it might take a miracle to bring Jenefer back to his arms, loving him again, trusting him again, eager for a second chance of the happiness he was sure they could find together. She was warm, kind, generous—but it wasn't love that glowed in her hazel eyes as she looked up at him, Blake knew. Only compassion for a man who had been through the mill.

'Is that what Mark needs? A miracle?' Her heart sank slightly.

'I won't know the full extent of the problem until he's on the operating table. By the way, where's Lucy? Shouldn't *she* be playing the part of ministering angel?'

'She's on duty in the Cardiac Unit all day. I'm standing in for her,' Jenefer replied with an attempt at lightheartedness.

Blake returned Mark's chart to its hook. 'You seem to be making a habit of doing that,' he commented dryly.

She shot him a wrathful look. What a chameleon he was! Charming her one moment, slapping her down

the next! A girl never knew where she was with Blake
Armstrong, she thought bitterly. In some ways, he
hadn't changed at all in six years.

Blake strolled towards the door. 'Have Dawson's
family been notified?'

Jenefer followed him out to the corridor. 'His
mother and a sister live in Scotland. I met them when
they were down here on holiday last year, so I spoke
to them myself. They're driving down and won't be
here before late afternoon.'

He nodded. 'We can't wait. I regard it as an
emergency,' he said bluntly. 'As you know them,
perhaps you could be on hand when they arrive?
Explain the situation, give them some tea and hold
their hands while he's in theatre?'

'I can leave that to Lucy! I'd rather be on hand to
assist you, Blake!'

'I'm afraid that isn't possible.'

Jenefer was annoyed by the sweeping dismissal.
'Why not? I could scrub for you. I'm an experienced
theatre nurse,' she said with a hint of indignation.

'I'm sure you are, but . . .'

'Theatres are short-staffed at weekends and those
who are on duty will be rushed off their feet, as usual.
I could be useful . . .'

'Not when your emotions are so involved.' The firm
tone cut across her persuasions.

Jenefer drew herself up to her full height. 'I'm a
trained nurse,' she reminded him, stiff with pride.
'You don't need to worry about my emotions, Blake.
Mark will be just another patient once he's on the
operating table. I've done a lot of theatre work and
I'm familiar with most procedures, and I know I can
do a good job.'

Blake shook his head, adamant. 'No.'

She bit her lip. Why didn't he understand how important it was to her to do something to help Mark? After all, it was partly her fault that he had to undergo such delicate and dangerous surgery.

'Why?' she persisted. 'I want to help and I'm well qualified to do so!' With an effort, she conquered rising indignation. Losing her temper wouldn't help Mark's situation or improve her relationship with Blake, she told herself sensibly. She put a tentative hand on the surgeon's arm. 'Please, Blake . . . it means a great deal to me.'

Blake sighed and succumbed. It was difficult for him to deny the lovely Jenefer anything she wanted, he admitted ruefully. If she was familiar with theatre procedure then she could probably make herself useful if only as a spare dirty nurse. 'I think I'm making a mistake, but . . . yes, all right. You can get into greens and watch,' he conceded. 'But that's all, Jenefer. You definitely aren't scrubbing for me, qualified or not!'

Jenefer smiled.

She smiled at him again when he walked into the operating-theatre some time later to find her gowned and gloved and busily laying out the instruments he would need for the operation on Dawson. There was a hint of triumph in her warm hazel eyes.

Blake glowered. 'What the hell do you think you're doing?' he demanded, angry that she thought she could ignore his ruling.

'Getting things ready.' Her eyes met and held his scowling gaze. 'Don't frown, Blake.' She lowered her voice as curious glances were shot at them by busy theatre nurses. 'There isn't anyone else available at the moment. Everyone's busy with a motorway pile-up and you said that Mark's case was urgent. I do know what I'm doing. I won't let you down.'

'Are you scrubbing for us, Jenefer? That's great!'
Called from the golf course to assist with the
emergency craniotomy, Barry Rowe strolled into the
operating-room on the enthusiastic words. Jenefer
smiled at him gratefully. 'Theatres haven't been the
same since you deserted us for the wards,' he went on.
Turning to Blake, he added: 'Jenefer's a marvellous
instrument nurse, you know. I always tell her she
ought to have been a surgeon. She has the hands for
it.'

Those hands went on working as Blake began to
discuss procedure with his junior surgeon. He was
forced to admit defeat and didn't like it, Jenefer
suspected, recognising the tension of anger in his tall
frame. Like herself, he was quick-tempered and
proud, and no doubt that was why they had once
quarrelled so bitterly and with such lasting results.

Mark was wheeled into the room, accompanied by
the duty anaesthetist, and she dismissed the intrusive
memories as she shook out sterile drapes. Recalling
how recently she had watched Blake operate on Hilda
Maitland and envied Stella Stead at his side, she
thought wryly that she hadn't expected to be assisting
him herself at any time, let alone so soon.

True to her word, she forgot everything but her
responsibility to surgeon and patient as she slapped
the scalpel into his waiting hand at the start of the
operation. Mark was no longer a young doctor that
she knew and liked when he wasn't drunk and
behaving like an idiot but merely another patient in
need of Blake's skill.

The atmosphere was tense as they worked together
beneath overhead lights, combining expertise with
efficiency. Now and again, a helpful Barry prompted

Jenefer if her hand seemed to hesitate over the array of instruments, but for the most part she knew just what was required, and anticipated so well that Blake was surprised at times into a nod of approval or the gleam of a smile in the dark eyes above the mask.

She surprised herself too, for it was months since her spell in Theatres. Perhaps she had missed her way, after all. Maybe she should have stuck to theatre work and then she would have seen a great deal of Blake now that he had turned up at Pagett's—and maybe that would have been a mistake too!

He was so confident, she thought admiringly, watching his strong hands working with slow precision as he navigated the network of nerves and tissues and tiny veins to find the subdural haematoma that had shown up on the scan. Once he had found it, he removed the clot and sealed the still-leaking haemorrhage with diathermy needle and microscopic ligature before irrigating the artery with Ringer's solution.

Barry checked pupils and reflexes and the anaesthetist confirmed that all was well with Mark's breathing and blood pressure and heart rhythm, then gave the go-ahead for the surgeon to sew up.

'There may be some slight damage to the nerve, but he's a healthy young man and ought to make a full recovery,' Blake said confidently.

'You must be relieved to hear that, Jenefer.' Barry smiled at the slender girl in the voluminous theatre gown, knowing her anxiety and its cause.

'I am, of course.' Jenefer wondered if there was anyone at Pagett's who *didn't* know that Mark Dawson had made a pass at her and been rebuffed with violence! 'Can we get a message to Lucy, do you think? She must be so anxious . . .' *She* felt badly enough about the whole business and she could sympathise with her friend's feelings in spite of the way that Lucy had rounded on her.

'Better wait,' Blake advised. 'He isn't out of the wood yet.' He looked across the table at Jenefer. 'Time enough for messages when he's in Recovery. You've done very well, but we haven't finished yet, Sister. Suture, please . . .'

It was all the praise she would get from him, Jenefer knew. But the warmth in his dark eyes had made her heart leap.

Later, leaving the theatre staff to clean up and sterilise used instruments, she followed the surgeon into the scrub annexe to untie the strings of his gown. Barry had left at the earliest possible moment to return to the golf course and his unfinished round.

'Thanks.' Blake pulled off his stained gown and dropped it into the dirty bin. Like most surgeons after demanding but successful surgery, he was still on a high, every sense sharpened, every perception tuned to a fine pitch, emotions running close to the surface. In such a mood, he liked to play a fierce game of squash, or swim several lengths, or run a few miles. Or make love. They were all good ways to unwind, he had found—and the last was the most attractive, if the least likely at the moment, he thought wryly, cap following the gown into the bin.

He bent over a basin and sluiced cold water over face and head to cool the fever in his blood. He needed the release that lovemaking could bring, and he had never wanted any woman as he wanted the one who stood watching and waiting, a towel for him in her hand.

Jenefer had always been special, he admitted. Cheryl had come a poor second to the girl with the bright chestnut curls and gravely pretty face, although he had cared enough to ensure that she never knew it. He had never cheated on his wife, but maybe that was only because Jenefer had no longer been around to quicken desire and compound love.

Blake took the towel from her with a fleeting smile that stirred her heart with its enchantment. Jenefer welled with the emotion that she had been denying ever since they knelt together beside Mark's unconscious body on Lucy's apology for a lawn.

Gleaming drops of water clung to the black curls that sprang from his temples and clustered at the nape of his neck. The deep V of his tunic exposed a triangle of powerful chest, more crisply curling black hair that invited a woman's touch. Broad shoulders and muscular thighs strained the seams of thin theatre greens. Darkly handsome, magnificently male, he filled her with a sudden longing for his embrace. She was swamped by the memory of his splendid and powerful lovemaking and her own eager response to it, and something in Blake's eyes as they encountered her own told her that he was remembering too.

For a moment she was riveted, heart thudding, desiring yet dreading a touch or a word or a smile to which she would instinctively respond and expose herself as a woman in love. Then, with an effort, she broke the spell, moving away and tugging at the strings of her own gown with slightly unsteady hands.

'Let me . . .' Blake's long fingers were cool against her neck. He unravelled the tangle of strings and then his hands slid along to her shoulders and gripped them gently. It took every ounce of his self-control to stop himself from sweeping her into his arms. 'Are you OK?' he asked softly. 'You're trembling.'

For a moment Jenefer revelled in the luxury of his

touch and the comfort of his closeness, yearning to turn into his arms and lift her face for his kiss and know again the joy of being desired by the only man she had ever loved. At eighteen, she hadn't hesitated. But now, six years later, her cautious heart warned her against repeating past mistakes.

She drew away. 'Reaction,' she said brightly. 'After boasting about my brilliance as a scrub nurse I've been absolutely terrified of doing the wrong thing.'

'And you've been very anxious about Dawson, haven't you?' Blake was sympathetic, a kindly glow in the smiling dark eyes.

'Well, I certainly didn't sleep much last night, I must admit. I felt so responsible . . .' She broke off as emotion almost overwhelmed her. She was tired and Blake's tenderness was suddenly even more unnerving than his nearness.

'A very natural reaction. But you made amends with your splendid performance as scrub nurse this morning. It seems a pity that you opted for ward work, as Rowe says. You and I might have made a splendid team, Jenefer.'

'I thought that was the original plan,' she said dryly, unable to resist the reminder of a disappointment that had nothing to do with her nursing career.

Catching the implication of the words, Blake met the challenge in her hazel eyes with a wry smile. 'Reproaching me? You broke our engagement,' he reminded her steadily.

'You didn't leave me any choice! Or should I have said nothing while you paraded another girl in front of all our friends? That would have set a precedent for the rest of our lives!'

'You might have checked your facts before you accused me of cheating. I was dating Cheryl before you came on the scene, in fact. As soon as I met you, she was wiped right off the map as far as I was concerned.'

'But not for long, apparently,' Jenefer snapped, but she felt that if she had known at the time that the other girl had first claim to Blake she might have accepted and forgiven his change of mind instead of nursing a bruised heart all these years.

'There were . . . complications.' He hesitated. 'I suppose you knew that she was Jake's granddaughter?'

Jenefer hadn't known. She was abruptly filled with a contempt that effectively nipped in the bud the new flowering of that love from long ago.

She looked at him coldly. 'It all becomes crystal clear,' she declared scathingly. 'I didn't stand a chance against that kind of competition, obviously. I knew you were ambitious, but I didn't think you'd go to those lengths to get what you wanted!'

On that sardonic note, she stalked out of the room and past the huddle of curious nurses who had probably heard every word.

Balling a fist, Blake slammed it furiously into the palm of his other hand. He was getting nowhere—messing it up completely! Jenefer saw herself as a woman scorned and anger still burned bright, and it was possible that she would never forgive him.

How could he expect her to understand that an ambitious surgeon had reached a crossroads in his life where he had felt compelled to choose between love and his career? He had made the wrong choice—and it seemed that he was still paying the price.

CHAPTER TEN

EMERGING into the dusk of a damp evening, Jenefer walked across the car park to where her small brown Fiat gleamed wetly beneath the amber lights. In Recovery, Mark was making all the right responses that indicated he had come out of coma. Although he wasn't fully round from the anaesthetic, she could relax in the knowledge that he was probably going to be all right, she thought thankfully.

Sliding behind the wheel, she turned the key in the ignition. Nothing happened. Frowning, she tried again. There wasn't a spark of response, no flicker of life in the headlights. She sighed. The car was overdue for a service, but she had put it off because she doubted that she could afford the extensive repairs it might need.

She knew nothing about the Fiat's innards, but she got out and lifted the bonnet to peer hopefully at the engine and its accoutrements. Out of the corner of her eye she saw the approach of a tall, powerfully built figure and knew before she turned that it was Blake.

'Having trouble?'

'Nothing I can't handle,' she returned with pride, and poked around the base of a spark plug as if she knew exactly what to do.

Blake watched with a glint of amusement in his dark eyes. 'A woman of our time, aren't you? Too independent to need a man for anything.'

Jenefer wisely decided to admit defeat. 'Do you understand cars?'

'Rather better than I understand women,' he said dryly.

She shot him a glowering look, but stepped back from the Fiat. 'Then perhaps you can tell me what's wrong.' She was sharp because she hated having to ask him for anything . . . playing into his hands, she thought irritably, and didn't stop to wonder why he was so consistently nice to her when she was consistently nasty to him.

Blake tinkered with wiring and leads while she stood in the chilly drizzle of the lowering dusk. 'Dead battery,' he diagnosed after several unsuccessful attempts to start the engine.

'It can't be! It was perfectly all right this morning,' she protested.

'Sure? It didn't splutter and cough before turning over?'

'Well, yes. But it's done that for days. It's inclined to be temperamental . . .'

'Much like its owner.' Blake closed down the bonnet. 'You'll have to leave it here for the night and get a local garage to sort it out tomorrow. Lock it up and I'll run you home.'

'I'll get a taxi. I wouldn't dream of giving you the trouble of taking me home.'

'Or the pleasure?' he said wryly. He put an apparently casual hand to the tumbling chestnut curls that glinted in the light from the lamp. 'You're getting wet while we argue, Jenefer.'

She backed from the touch of his hand. 'I'm not arguing. It's just that there's no point in taking you out of your way.'

'It isn't out of my way, and there's no point in ringing for a taxi when there's a car and a very willing chauffeur at your service. I'm not going to kidnap you, for heaven's sake,' he added with a disarming smile.

'Oh, all right . . .' It was ungracious because she was cross with herself for melting before the warmth of his charm. His smile, his touch, his very presence at Pagett's were a growing threat to the uncomplicated life she had built for herself, and she was determined to resist it. Loving him had only brought her heartache. Why should it be any different this time?

Sitting at his side in the sleekly purring Jaguar, she was alarmingly aware of his impact on her heightened senses, nevertheless. She saw nothing of the wet streets, the passing cars, the people on the pavements. Staring through the rain-spattered windscreen at the ribbon of road as they drove towards the town centre, she only saw his handsome face and dancing eyes and the smile that snatched at her heart.

He had slotted a cassette into the music centre and she wondered if it was only coincidence that a well-known group played all the tunes to which they had once danced and sung and made love. More memories to haunt and taunt her with the might-have-been . . .

Blake's nearness, the music and the memories were lulling her into a susceptible frame of mind, she realised, hardening the heart that was dangerously close to trusting him again.

Was he really trying to turn back the clock? Did he really want her again—or was it just impossible for a sensual man like Blake to accept that she no longer wanted him?

He brought the powerful car to a halt outside the house and the music came to an abrupt end as he switched off the engine. Jenefer turned in her seat, meaning to thank him and wish him goodnight. Before she could speak, he leaned towards her and brushed her lips with his own, so lightly that there was really no need for her to rear back as if she had been stung.

'*Don't!*' she exploded.

Undeterred, Blake reached to cradle her furious face in both strong hands, smiling into her stormy eyes. 'Come on, Jenny,' he coaxed softly. 'What we did to each other was a long time ago. This is *now*. Enjoy it . . .' With a long finger, he traced the delicate curve of her lips and then followed the caressing trail with the warm pressure of his mouth.

Jenefer tensed. Her lips were as cold and smooth as marble, but her heart leapt in wild response and her body quivered at the onslaught on her senses. It took all her resolution not to wind her arms about his neck and give herself up to the magic in his kiss.

Blake stroked the bright curls with a tender hand and then buried his face in their perfumed silk, drawing her close. 'I missed you,' he murmured, thinking how inadequate the words were to convey the ache of longing that had never really left him.

Jenefer pulled away, angry. 'Do you expect me to believe that? When you never *phoned*—or *wrote*—or *anything*!' All the hurt of days and weeks and months of waiting for some sign of caring that never came throbbed in her voice.

'I had my reasons . . .'

'Of course you did! Cheryl!'

'She was pregnant,' Blake said baldly.

'Oh!' The revelation was a dash of cold water across her face. She swallowed. 'Someone was careless,' she commented with uncharacteristic flippancy.

Blake frowned. 'I was fond of her, but I hadn't made any promises. I played it straight, Jenefer—told her about you, that you were special. She seemed to take it pretty well. I had no idea that she was pregnant when I asked you to marry me, of course.'

'Oh, I don't know,' Jenefer said in a hard tone. 'Proposing was probably just a ploy to get me into bed.'

'You know better than that,' he said brusquely.

'I thought I did!'

Blake put a hand beneath her chin and turned her face so that she was compelled to meet the intent glow in his eyes. 'I was very much in love with you.'

Past tense, Jenefer thought heavily. But she had known that for long enough, surely? 'That's why you went ahead and married Cheryl,' she agreed dryly, moving from his touch, stilling the wild beat of her heart.

'She threatened all sorts of things if I didn't. Having me thrown out of Hartlake was only part of it.'

'Losing your chance of the consultancy mattered far more than losing me, obviously,' Jenefer jibed. 'And I thought you'd married her because she was sick and you were sorry for her!' Deliberately, she whipped him with her contempt.

Blake sighed. 'She *was* sick, but no one knew that until she lost the baby a few weeks after we were married.'

Unexpectedly, Jenefer was swamped by a wave of compassion. 'Poor girl,' she said quietly, tears pricking her eyes. 'She was dealt a really rotten hand, wasn't she? A husband who didn't love her, a baby who didn't live and then the discovery that she had an incurable blood disease!'

'She was a lovely and courageous girl and I was very fond of her. We had nearly five years together, and she was happy—I made sure of that,' Blake said tautly. 'But perhaps you understand now why I couldn't step into Jake's shoes as everyone expected and he wished?

He decided to retire when Cheryl died, and I felt that her life was the price of the consultancy that I'd wanted and worked for all those years.'

It was hard not to put her arms about him, although neither tone nor manner invited her sympathy. He had come to terms with grief and guilt long since, she realised . . . and feeling sorry for a man could lead to all kinds of dangerous complications, Jenefer warned herself sensibly.

'Things haven't been so easy for you either,' she said stiffly.

Blake shrugged. 'Oh, they've improved a lot since I came to work at Pagett's,' he assured her in lighter vein. 'I like the job and the people—and meeting you again is a bonus.'

She had been too encouraging, Jenefer thought in sudden panic. He did think that they were about to pick up where they had left off! If he once thought that she was weakening, ready to forgive and forget and start again, he would give her no peace until they were lovers once more—and then she might find it impossible to live without him! He would string her along while it suited him—and probably end up marrying someone else. Ann Morley, for instance! Well, she wasn't having any of it. She wasn't going to lay her heart at his feet for him to trample on all over again!

'Meeting again is just one of those things that happen, and it isn't going to lead anywhere, Blake,' she said firmly.

Smiling, he reached for her hand and carried it to his lips. 'I know you find it hard to admit, but we belong, Jenefer. We took a wrong turning, that's all. It brought us both to the same place in the end, and maybe that's destiny. So why fight it?'

Jenefer withdrew her hand. 'It's a long time since I thought of you as my destiny, Blake. You obviously haven't heard that I'm engaged to be married.' It was cool and so confident that it was convincing.

Blake's eyes narrowed. 'That item of news does appear to have escaped me,' he drawled. 'Is it true?'

She laughed. 'Why should I lie to you? I don't have to invent a fiancé to keep the wolves from my door!' she said lightly.

'Who is he?' Blake struggled with a fierce and bitter jealousy, an acute disappointment, for the hope of finding Jenefer still free, of winning back her love and her trust, of eventually persuading her to marry him had borne him through the difficult months since Cheryl's death and his departure from Hartlake. He had kept tabs on Jenefer's whereabouts for years through mutual friends and relied on them to keep him informed of her relationships with other men. It seemed that they had let him down.

'Oh, you wouldn't know him,' Jenefer assured him airily. 'He isn't a medical man. They tend to make unreliable lovers, I've found.'

Blake tapped her bare left hand. 'Can't he afford to give you an engagement ring?'

'Of course he can! He's a chartered accountant with his own company and he's doing very well, in fact. I didn't want a ring. One experience of a formal engagement was quite enough! Not many people know that we're engaged either. It's a mistake to tell people too much, I've found. One feels such a fool when things go wrong.'

Blake didn't believe her. Or was it only that he didn't want to believe? He had seen the way that Ryan Montague looked at Jenefer. He had heard other men speak of her with a mixture of admiration and respect.

She was the kind of woman that any man might want for a wife—and he couldn't blame Jenefer for preferring a husband who wasn't in the medical profession, he thought wryly. A layman could give her so much more of his time and interest and energy. But no man could love her more than he did.

'When are you getting married?'

'We haven't set the date yet, but it will be soon. A very quiet wedding, of course—Tom hates fuss and so do I.' Jenefer never told lies, but these were tripping off her tongue with consummate ease. Somehow she had to make Blake understand that whatever had once been between them was really finished and could never happen again! And they were the kind of lies that could soon be turned into truth, for Tom did want to marry her and she had finally made up her mind.

'Then I can only say that I wish you every happiness,' Blake said stonily.

'Thanks very much.' Smiling, Jenefer reached to open the door. 'And thanks for bringing me home, Blake.' Smiling, she got out of the car. Smiling, she turned to wave a casual farewell as the Jaguar slid away from the kerb. Smiling, she let herself into the flat and closed the door—and then she stood with her back to the panels and let the tears flow.

She wept as she had never wept even in the first days of heartbreak. She wasn't crying for a lost opportunity, of course. Only for lost dreams, cherished much too long.

At least she still had her pride, she comforted herself when the sobbing eased and the tears began to dry. If she had gone into Blake's arms in the way that heart and wilful body prompted that pride would have been lost for ever. For no self-respecting woman allowed a man to make a fool of her twice—and only a fool would trust Blake Armstrong with his smiling eyes and smooth tongue and sensuous appeal.

By the time that Tom telephoned to tell her that he was home and looking forward to seeing her soon, Jenefer was in control of her emotions once more and even more determined to take the necessary step that would put Blake out of her life completely and for ever.

Tom made up for having forgotten her birthday by taking her out to dinner. 'I like your dress,' he approved. 'Very chic.' Leaning back in his chair, he smiled at her as the smoke from his cigar wreathed about his head.

Jenefer smiled back at him, pleased by the compliment. He so seldom remarked on what she wore, how she looked, assuming that his admiration was tacit because he sought her company. She felt that the black dress with the silver slashes, newest in her wardrobe and worn only once before, was very suitable for the occasion, even if she was slightly underdressed when compared to the other women in their furs and diamonds and haute-couture gowns.

The Excelsior was a very exclusive country club on the coast road, and she didn't care to think what it must be costing Tom to entertain her so royally, even though she knew that he could well afford it. She wondered if it was the right setting for the scene that she must soon steel herself to enact. But Tom was in mellow mood and she might never have a better opportunity.

She wasn't about to marry Tom just to spite Blake, of course. She was very fond of Tom. Perhaps, deep down, she had unconsciously been waiting for another Blake to come into her life—or even the same Blake, in her wildest dreams. But the Blakes of this world were not very reliable. It was time she thought about a husband, home and children—and Tom would make a very good husband, she told herself firmly.

But how on earth did a girl steer the conversation round to the subject of marriage without being too blatant about it?

Jenefer thought of an opening gambit and then promptly lost courage. 'You haven't said much about your trip,' she said instead. 'Was it a success?'

'Reasonably so. I won't bore you with the details,' Tom returned smoothly.

'But you enjoyed it?'

'The weather wasn't very kind.'

'So much for the golf and the long walks that you planned,' she sympathised. She thought he looked tired, more gaunt than usual. But he was relaxed, buoyant, even rather pleased with himself . . . the cat who had been at the cream, Jenefer thought suddenly, wondering a little. It must have been a very successful few days in the Lake District, one way or another, for Tom to have come home in such ebullient mood.

'I managed a round or two.' Looking beyond her, Tom raised a hand in brief acknowledgement of an acquaintance among a party of new arrivals. Jenefer half turned in her seat. 'Max Morley,' he obliged. 'Our local philanthropist and a very valuable client. You must know the name. It's to be seen all over Penfold and the surrounding areas. Morley Stores, Morley Mouldings, Morley Marine . . .'

Jenefer wasn't really listening, her gaze riveted on the tall, dinner-jacketed man escorting the blonde girl in the stunning scarlet sheath through the tables in the wake of the millionaire businessman who had a finger in almost every pie in Penfold.

The man was Blake, the pretty girl hanging on his

arm and laughing up at him and behaving as if he belonged to her was Ann Morley.

'. . . and something that will interest *you*, Jenefer,' Tom went on. 'He's planning to build a private hospital in the near future—the first of its kind in the area. To be called the Morley Clinic, no doubt,' he added dryly, for the man's conceit was notorious, although he had good reason to be proud of all that he had done for Penfold and he was generous with time and interest as well as money. 'I expect you recognise Giles Lomax, Penfold's Member of Parliament?' He hesitated. 'And his wife, of course. I don't know the other couple. The girl is very striking, isn't she?'

'She's the new junior on my ward. I don't know if there's a connection, but her name is Morley too. Ann Morley,' Jenefer said stiffly.

'Then that must be the daughter.' Tom glanced at the girl in the red dress with more interest. 'I've never met her, but I've heard Max talk about her at times. A very independent young woman who doesn't have much to do with her family, apparently. I didn't know she was home or that she was interested in nursing. Perhaps she thinks training will make her eligible for a key post in her father's clinic when it opens.'

'Probably.' Jenefer felt sick. Max Morley's daughter! No wonder Blake was taking so much interest in the girl. Perhaps his ambition was geared these days to becoming star surgeon at the Morley Clinic when it eventually opened—even if he had to marry the founder's daughter to secure that aim! It wouldn't be the first time he had allowed ambition to rule his life, after all. It seemed to Jenefer's heavy heart that he was prepared to sacrifice anything and anybody on the altar of success.

'Is that the husband?' Tom asked curiously.

'No. She isn't married.' *Yet*, Jenefer amended silently. 'That's Blake Armstrong, the neuro-surgeon who operated on Hilda Maitland the other day. She's doing very well, by the way. She should be coming back to the ward within a few days.'

It was an attempt to change the subject, but Tom wasn't ready to be diverted. He watched Nicola through sharply narrowed eyes as she leaned across the table to speak to the surgeon, to smile at him, to issue an unmistakable invitation with the subtle body language that she used so successfully on most men. Including himself . . .

'The kind of man that all the women go for, I suppose,' he said brusquely. He forced a smile as Jenefer looked at him curiously. 'I expect all your junior nurses are throwing their caps at him.'

'A few.' Ann Morley in particular, she thought bitterly—and that cap was the one that Blake had rushed to pick up. Now she knew why!

Had Blake known that she was Max Morley's daughter and welcomed the warm encouragement in the new junior's smile—or had they known each other before either of them came to work at Pagett's?

Oh, of course! She had been blind, stupid! Ryan had remarked on their behaviour in the Winchester Arms and asked if they were old friends, she recalled. They must have met in London—possibly when his wife was still alive. Ann had known about Cheryl, had seemed upset when she spoke about Blake's wife . . . so had she been *Cheryl's* friend, in fact? Had it seemed the most natural thing in the world to Blake that he should turn to his wife's best friend for comfort when he became a widower?

So no doubt it was *Ann* who had brought him to Penfold and to Pagett's—Ann and her millionaire father's plan to build a private hospital in the area!

Jenefer knew she was an idiot to have imagined even for a moment that *she* was the attraction. Blake might desire her still, but he had an eye to the main chance as always, she thought contemptuously, thankful that she hadn't melted into his arms at the first opportunity.

Ann Morley was welcome to him.

She meant to marry Tom. As soon as it could be arranged.

CHAPTER ELEVEN

'THIS is so nice.' Jenefer touched Tom's hand to recapture the attention that had strayed once more to the nearby table. 'I'm really enjoying the evening, Tom.'

'I'm glad . . .' The words were absent, like his smile. He was watching jealously to see if Nicola was taking an interest in Blake Armstrong in spite of the husband who guarded her so possessively but had been coaxed by her silver tongue and winning ways into approving her trip to the Lake District to visit a sick cousin.

They *were* cousins, if many times removed, and he *was* sick, Tom told himself wryly. Lovesick. Sick of trying to convince Nicola that her happiness lay with him. Sick of wanting, of waiting, of watching their lives slip away without each other. Well, he had finally won. His beautiful wife might be a valuable asset to Giles Lomax, but it was one he was soon destined to lose, Tom thought with satisfaction.

Those idyllic few days among the superb splendour of lakes and hills and woodland had ended with Nicola's promise to marry him as soon as she had got a divorce. It would take a little time, of course. In the meantime, they needed to be as discreet as before about their meetings, their feelings, their plans for the future.

However, knowing that the Lomaxes were dining with Max Morley at the Excelsior that evening, Tom had been unable to resist the lure of being in the same surroundings with the woman he loved—and Jenefer

136

was a useful camouflage on this occasion as on so
many others, although she was unaware of the fact.

She was saying something to him and he turned
with a courteous inclination of his head, forcing
himself to take in the words.

'. . . patient with me all these months, and I do
appreciate it, Tom. You're so considerate and very
understanding. Any woman would think herself lucky
to be your wife, I feel. I've decided that I'd like very
much to marry you. Let's set a date, shall we? Soon,
please. I feel that we've lost too much time as it is . . .'

Jenefer had plunged into speech before she could
change her mind. The sight of Blake making up to a
millionaire's daughter only a short distance away was
all the incentive she needed to secure her own future
in which he could not possibly play any part. Even if
he wished to do so.

Successful business-men who learned a great many
secrets in the process of unearthing the financial
affairs and tax liabilities of their clients seldom
showed surprise or dismay. Tom was no exception.
But beneath the calm exterior lurked shock and horror
and a desperate need to recall exactly what he had said
to Jenefer all those weeks ago.

'I really don't know what to say . . .' He was lost for
words for perhaps the only time in his life. It was
going to be the hardest thing he had ever done to dash
that shining sparkle from her hazel eyes, to dispel the
happiness that showed itself in the tremble of her soft
mouth, the slight flush in her lovely face, the
eagerness in her slender body.

'You could say that you're pleased, that it's what
you wanted most in the world,' Jenefer teased, never
doubting that was how he felt even if unexpected
delight at her decision had robbed him of his usual

cool composure.

'I'm very flattered, naturally . . .'

'You're much too modest, Tom. You're a catch and you know it!' She had to resort to levity or she might disgrace herself by bursting into tears. She had burned her boats and there was no going back—and nothing for her if she did, in any case. Certainly not Blake, with his ambitious plans for the future that had never really included her even when he was claiming to love her.

Tom smiled, aware of dry lips and a mind that scurried in four directions at once in search of an escape. He didn't want to hurt Jenefer. She was a lovely girl and a very good friend. But this talk of marriage must be knocked on the head as soon as possible. For if Nicola got to hear of it . . .!

It was entirely his own fault, he realised. In a despairing moment when he felt that Nicola had no intention of leaving Lomax for him or any other man, he had heard himself suggesting to Jenefer that they should get married. He hadn't really meant it and he had almost forgotten the proposal that she had obviously been reluctant to consider, much to his relief. Now he was appalled to learn that she had neither forgotten nor dismissed the suggestion and was ready to make plans, to set a date, to notify all their friends.

'This calls for champagne, surely?' Jenefer swept on brightly, a little wildly, having already drunk far more than she usually did to get her through the ordeal of throwing herself at Tom's head.

She wondered why she saw it in that light. For Tom *wanted* to marry her, had said so, had implied it in a hundred different ways. For one awful moment Jenefer wondered if she had got it all wrong, if Tom had never meant that proposal of marriage or had changed his mind or had fallen in love with someone else in the meantime.

Having told Blake that she was engaged to Tom Cornell, she *had* to make it happen! Tom was such a cold man, so undemonstrative and unemotional and passionless. He *was* pleased, of course. He just couldn't show it or express his feelings in words like other men.

She had often thought about the many emotions that must be locked away in that dispassionate breast and wondered if any woman held the key. Well, when she was his wife, it would fall to her to release the real man behind all that ice—and once over that hurdle she might quite like being married to Tom.

Sparkling, vivacious, drawing attention to herself and apparently revelling in it, she was not at all the reserved and rather private person that he knew, Tom thought wryly, wondering why she had suddenly set her heart on marrying him. She had always seemed so dedicated to nursing that he had often doubted that she would marry at all. There were women who needed husband, home and children. Jenefer had never seemed to be one of them. Until now.

He reached for the restless hands that were everywhere, fingering an ear-ring, touching a stray curl, toying with the silk of her dress, moving the empty wine-glass from one place to another.

'Champagne? On top of all that wine? Do you think that's wise?' he asked lightly, playing for time while he ransacked his brain for the words to make it clear that he had no wish to hurt her but no desire to marry her either.

Jenefer laughed. 'Do you think I'm drunk? I *am*! Drunk with happiness. I can't wait to marry you—and

I'm sorry that I took so long to make up my mind. Thank heavens you cared enough to wait!' She leaned to kiss him full on the mouth. 'I *do* love you,' she declared defiantly.

The ring of the words reached Blake, too aware of the couple who gazed into each other's eyes, held hands, smiled and kissed like the lovers they obviously were. He could no longer doubt Jenefer's claim to be engaged to the man.

He wanted to tear Tom Cornell apart with his bare hands. He wanted to seize Jenefer and throw her over his shoulder like a caveman of old and run off with her to some private place far from this lavish club-house with its stereotyped characters who probably knew nothing about love and the way it could take over a man's whole being. He wanted to take her and make her his own once more—and this time for all eternity.

His feelings were primitive and powerful and must be kept firmly under control, he knew. For Jenefer had the right to love where she wished and there was nothing he could do to stop her marrying the man she had chosen. He had long since forfeited his right to any say in what she did with her life.

Ann met his sombre eyes, understanding and sympathy in her smile. 'I'm sorry,' she murmured under cover of reaching for a dropped napkin. 'I'm as surprised as you are.'

She had made it her business to find out all she could about Jenefer Gale, but she had obviously been misinformed about the Ward Sister's relationship with a local business-man. She had known Blake since he had married her closest friend. She thought him the kindest and most caring man she had ever known and felt that he deserved to be happy after the bad years with Cheryl. She wasn't in love with him or she might not have been so anxious to help him win back the girl he had given up to marry Cheryl.

Watching the slow decline of her dearest friend, Ann had resolved to return to her original dream of nursing. Her father was a generous contributor to the Pagett Foundation Hospital in Penfold and her mother was on several of its committees, so it seemed a natural choice for her training.

She had encouraged Blake to try for the job of senior surgical registrar to the NSU at Pagett's, invited him to stay at Morley Manor until he found a flat or a house to suit him in the neighbourhood, taken him to places where he might run into Jenefer and introduced him to people who were Jenefer's friends, and done what she could to further his cause with the Ward Sister without being too obvious about it.

Now it seemed that they had both been wasting their time.

Tom felt trapped. Casting around him for a way out of the dilemma, he met Nicola's hard gaze and did his best to convey without words that it was all a mistake. She looked away, her lip curling. He began to feel quite ill. Things had been going so well and now it had all blown up in his face—and all because he had relied on Jenefer's commonsense outlook and his own conviction that she found nothing in him to love.

He signalled to the waiter to bring the bill for signature, suddenly consumed with a passionate fury at his own stupidity and Jenefer's understandable expectations. 'Let's go,' he said urgently, surging to his feet. 'We need to talk about this in private.'

Jenefer was alarmed by the forceful tone, the determined expression in his eyes, the unexpected hint of passion in the man who towered above her. Unsure of his reactions, she had deliberately chosen the protection of a public restaurant to tell him that she would marry him. Now she felt that in the privacy of his house or her flat she would be too vulnerable to a response that she might not be able to handle.

As Tom wrapped the fringed silk shawl about her shoulders with impatient hands, she wondered if she had unleashed those hidden but long suspected emotions. The cool, austere and reliably impersonal Tom suddenly seemed to be a very different animal.

Passing Max Morley's party, Tom was assailed by the man's booming voice. He paused reluctantly to shake hands. 'How are you, Max? Giles . . . Mrs Lomax . . .' He nodded to the MP and then his wife, careful not to meet Nicola's beautiful, accusing eyes.

Standing beside him, Jenefer slipped a hand through his arm in a gesture more defiant than possessive, chin on the tilt and a proud smile hovering about her lips. She had hoped to avoid this encounter, the confrontation with Blake's narrowed but inscrutable gaze, the uncomfortable feeling of guilt that surely didn't apply to the situation.

She wasn't letting Blake down, she reminded herself firmly. She was just making it clear to him and to everyone else that she was done with dreaming futile dreams about a star surgeon.

'I don't think I know this lovely young lady . . .' Max Morley eyed Jenefer with a mixture of curiosity and admiration that his wife would have disapproved if she had been present that evening. For Annabel Morley kept her warm-hearted and generous husband on a very tight rein.

'Oh, but you know all about Jenefer even if you haven't met, Dad,' Ann said lightly before Tom could attempt an introduction. 'I've talked about her a lot lately. She's the Sister in Charge of my ward at

Pagett's—and soon to be Mrs Tom Cornell, aren't you, Jenefer?' Her smile was warmer than the Ward Sister probably deserved, but Ann liked her enough to feel that maybe she couldn't help having fallen out of love with Blake. Six years was a long time, after all.

'Then you're a lucky man, Tom!' Max declared warmly, beaming at the news. 'And a dark horse to boot!'

'Congratulations, Cornell.' Giles Lomax raised his wine-glass in a smiling toast, his tone conveying none of the relief he felt that Nicola's penchant for the man would now come to nothing.

Tom felt as if he was riding on a roller-coaster. 'Nothing's settled . . .' he began in a desperate attempt to get off, reluctant to humiliate Jenefer but anxious to reassure Nicola and correct a general misunderstanding.

'We were just discussing a date for the wedding, in fact. Weren't we, Tom?' Hugging his arm, Jenefer smiled up at him even more defiantly, feeling the bore of dark eyes that she resolutely refused to meet, unaware that she was making matters worse for Tom by the moment. 'June is a nice month, I thought . . .'

'Oh, I do agree,' Nicola Lomax said lightly, her smile failing to dispel the glint of ice in the lovely sapphire eyes. 'Giles and I were married in June. On such a lovely day too. Happy the bride the sun shines on . . . isn't that the saying? More than true, in my case, I must say.'

'And very prettily said, my darling.' The MP lifted his wife's hand to his lips and kissed it.

Tom's mouth hardened into a grim line. 'I know you'll excuse me, Max,' he said brusquely. 'But Jenefer and I have a lot to discuss . . .' He hustled her through the tables, a jut to his jaw, silent until they were out in the open. Then he exploded. 'Damn it! Now it will be all over town that we're engaged to be married!'

'Does it matter?' Jenefer was puzzled by his anger, the tension in his tall frame. He didn't answer. As he strode towards his parked car with a discourtesy that she had never known in him, she hurried to catch up. 'Tom! What's wrong? Isn't it what you want? Don't you *want* to marry me?' she asked breathlessly on a sudden surge of hope that she could extricate herself from something she had regretted as soon as the words were spoken.

Tom turned at the urgent note in her lilting voice to see the stricken look in her lovely eyes and found it impossible to be honest—and what *did* it matter? Nicola was lost to him now, he knew. He had seen that in her eyes and heard it underlined in the incident with her husband.

She had probably never intended to leave Lomax, in any case. The idyllic weekend they had shared in the Lake District suddenly seemed to Tom to have been no more than an interlude to Nicola, while he had believed it to be the prelude to a future with the woman he loved.

Without Nicola, the future held very little for him, he thought heavily. So he might just as well marry Jenefer if that was what she wanted. She deserved so much more than he could give, but he could only do his best to make her happy.

'Oh, my dear!' Penitent, he caught her into his arms. 'I'm a brute to behave so badly, but you took me by surprise, you know.' He laid his cheek against her curls. 'God knows why you want to marry *me*. I don't deserve you.'

His mouth was hard, bruising her lips. His arms

were strong, crushing her breasts. But Jenefer sensed a lack of real passion in his embrace and felt relief. It would be easier to live with an innate coldness than to cope with a passion that insisted on invoking her own, she knew. To lie in Tom's arms and enjoy his lovemaking would still seem a betrayal of the kind of love that could come only once in a lifetime.

On the way to her flat, they made plans.

A June wedding, if that was Jenefer's choice, Tom agreed. A quiet affair with only family and close friends, Jenefer urged. A honeymoon in Greece. A public announcement of their engagement, of course—it would probably leak out anyway, Tom pointed out—and she must have a ring.

Recalling what she had said to Blake on the subject, Jenefer instantly demurred. 'Is that necessary, Tom? Nurses get out of the habit of wearing rings, you know. It will be more off than on.' The words were also a warning that she meant to carry on as Sister Cresswell, although she didn't think that would be a problem where Tom was concerned. He approved and admired women who combined marriage with a career.

'Nevertheless, it's expected, isn't it? The first thing that all your junior nurses will demand to see.' Tom smiled down at her indulgently. 'And I have the very thing, if you don't object—my mother's engagement ring.'

Jenefer swallowed an instinctive protest. She was using Tom to protect herself from the heartache and despair of loving another man. She owed him something—and if it would please him . . . 'I think that's a lovely idea,' she said brightly.

Tom patted her hand. 'My mother would have loved you, Jenefer.'

'And mine will be delighted with the news. She's always approved of you,' Jenefer told him with truth. 'Be prepared for a dinner invitation in the very near future, won't you?'

'I shall look forward to it.'

Heart thumping, Jenefer led the way into her flat and dumped bag and shawl on a chair. 'I expect you'd like a drink . . .?'

'No more for me, Jenefer. I daren't run the risk of being breathalysed.'

'Coffee, then?'

Tom shook his head. 'I'm awash with it now.'

Hearing a note of impatience, she looked up at her newly-acquired fiancé in sudden wariness, and came near to panic. In a moment, he would probably reach for her, claim her lips and demand the desired response to the passion she sensed in him. He had been so patient, so tolerant, so understanding all these months, but now she had given him the right to insist on the lovemaking that she had always avoided.

'I could do with a cup,' she said hastily, backing towards the kitchen. 'Make yourself at home while I switch on the percolator.'

Coming back into the room a few moments later, she found that he had lowered his tall frame to the shabby sofa, casting aside the brightly covered cushion at his back, for he was a man who disliked too much comfort. Hands behind his head, long legs stretched to their full length, he surveyed her living-room with a disparaging expression in his grey eyes.

'This won't be your home much longer, I'm glad to say,' he said abruptly. 'I know I own the place, but it isn't good enough for you, Jenefer.'

'I've been very happy here,' she returned defensively, looking around the room with its bright carpet and curtains and crammed bookshelves, its cheerful clutter of ornaments and photographs, its vases of colourful spring flowers in every corner. It *was* home to Jenefer and she loved it, and it would be a wrench to leave it.

She had never liked Tom's house, large and detached, set amid several acres in a remote part of Penfold. It was a cold and rather forbidding house that didn't seem lived in by anyone, impersonally if expensively furnished, seeming to lack the warmth and welcome of a home and devoid of a woman's touch, in spite of a very efficient housekeeper.

In some ways, Stonewalls reflected Tom's character and personality, Jenefer thought suddenly, realising how little she really knew about the man she was planning to marry—and discovering how little she *liked* him.

It was a shock.

Hastily she rejected such a nonsensical idea. Of course she liked Tom. She was fond of him. She trusted him. They got on very well and had much in common, liking the same things and the same people. He would be a very good husband and it would be her own fault if she wasn't happy as his wife, Jenefer told herself sternly.

She sat down at his side and smiled at him warmly to atone for the disloyal thoughts that he luckily hadn't discerned. 'Where were we? Athens, wasn't it? It should be beautiful in June.'

'Beautiful at any time of the year . . . like you, darling.' On the slightly stilted words, Tom put his arm about Jenefer and drew her towards him, smiling.

Jenefer wasn't aware of the forced tone, the rather strained smile, the effort he made to play the lover. She was steeling herself for his kiss, his tentative caresses that must surely lead to the lovemaking she dreaded.

He should have agreed to the champagne, she thought inconsquentially. She might have seen Tom and the prospect of marriage in a much rosier light. She might have gone into his arms in euphoric, excited eagerness such as he deserved. Instead, stone cold sober now, she knew that she was making a terrible mistake in marrying him—and she didn't know how to extricate herself without hurting him.

She just couldn't do it to Tom.

She knew too well the heartache and humiliation and agonising despair of a broken engagement and a lost love.

CHAPTER TWELVE

'I THINK it's time to start dialysis, Mrs Wilcox.' Keith Oliver, a renal physician with a number of patients presently on Cresswell, made a note on the chart and returned it carefully to its hook at the foot of the bed. He smiled kindly at the too-thin woman, sitting upright against her pillows, sallow of skin, dark-ringed eyes showing the yellowish tinge associated with chronic kidney disease. 'I'm afraid we can't afford to leave it any longer, in fact.'

It was the verdict that the patient had been both expecting and dreading, and her fingers closed convulsively over Jenefer's comforting hand. but she smiled and nodded. 'Whatever you say, Doctor. As long as it means that I can go home and just come in for treatment now and again.' She looked at him hopefully.

'Every other day, I'm afraid, my love.' He broke it to her gently. 'But that's better than having to stay in hospital all the time, isn't it?'

The patient bravely swallowed disappointment. 'Oh, I don't know about that, Doctor. It's been a nice rest and I won't get flowers and grapes and chocolates from my lot once I'm out of here!' she joked with the sense of humour that had brightened the days for staff and patients on Cresswell.

Keith grinned. 'Well, we won't send you home just yet. I want to see how you react to dialysis and we need to keep a careful eye on your blood urea count.' He turned to Jenefer. 'Do we have the latest figures, Sister?'

'Somewhere in the file . . . yes, here they are, Doctor.' Jenefer's tone was slightly absent as she turned from the trolley with the required piece of paper. A flash of white coat had caught her eye and a glance had confirmed that it was Blake, strolling back and forth at the end of the ward in leisurely manner, hands thrust into the pockets of immaculate silver-grey trousers, matching tie carefully knotted, thick dark curls brushed into neat submission over the proud, handsome head.

Jenefer stifled the instinctive flutter of her heart. She hadn't seen him since that night at the Excelsior. But she had learned that he was living at Morley Manor and rumours about his relationship with Max Morley's daughter were suddenly thick and fast. She had no reason to doubt any of them.

She saw Brenda Walsh hurry up to the surgeon. He smiled and shook his head and indicated that he was waiting to speak to the Ward Sister. Reluctantly the staff nurse returned to her patient.

Successful surgeon, triumphant male—a danger to any woman, Jenefer thought stonily, seeing him smile at a patient who passed him on a nurse's arm, heading for the day-room. She observed the woman's sudden confusion and the colour that rose in the first-year's face at the unexpected notice from a senior surgeon. She was abruptly reminded of herself at eighteen. Blake's powerful personality and dark good looks and the liquid charm of his smile had always been able to quicken any woman's pulses.

But not her own any more.

Briefly, crazily, she had imagined that she still loved him. The discovery that he had jilted her to marry Sir Jake's granddaughter with that coveted consultancy in mind, together with the realisation that he had taken

a job at Pagett's to further his ambitious hopes for the
future rather than to find her again, had brought her
abruptly to her senses. The swift return to sanity and
a need to know exactly where she stood had shown her
that Tom was her real security, her promise of real
and lasting happiness.

Jenefer stifled the instinctive, deep-down protest
that Tom was dull, prosaic, cold-blooded. If
excitement and adventure and passion meant a man
she couldn't trust with her heart or anything else then
she was glad to settle for Tom! She didn't deceive
herself that she loved him. But that would come in
time.

Just as Tom would eventually be the lover she
needed—warm and sensitive and sensual, knowing
just how to stir her to eager, excited response. In the
meantime, she welcomed the tepid lovemaking that
was so easily discouraged. In fact, it was a relief that
Tom wasn't urging her into bed, content to wait until
they were married. His restraint was in keeping with
all she knew of him and, until she could sort out the
confusion of her feelings, she was glad of it. But she
couldn't help quickening at the memory of Blake and
the natural, irresistible urgency of loving that had
swept aside everything but their passionate need of
each other and transported her to a heaven she might
never know again.

A man for every woman, it was said. Blake had
taken her and made her his own, and there were
moments when Jenefer felt she could never belong to
any other man. It would be awful if only Blake had the
power to make her tremble at a touch, to set her
senses on fire, to whirl her into that world of
enchantment and ecstasy with his kisses and caresses
and powerful, tender lovemaking. In six years she

hadn't experienced one ripple of desire for any man but Blake—and since he had come back into her life heart and mind and body were a continual tumult of longing and remembrance . . .

Jenefer wrenched her thoughts back to the present to realise that Keith was talking about the possibility of a kidney transplant for Mrs Wilcox, and a gleam of new hope had brightened the woman's thin face.

'First the bad news and then the good?' Jenefer smiled up at the physician as they strolled between the double row of beds towards the end of the ward, a few minutes later. She was aware that Blake was observing them with a hint of impatience, but she had no intention of hurrying Keith from the ward to suit an autocratic surgeon.

'The transplant? Well, I'll put her on the waiting list, anyway. I don't think dialysis is the long-term solution to her problems, so I hope it won't be long before a suitable donor can be found. You're in demand this morning, Sister,' he added with a jerk of his head at the waiting surgeon.

Jenefer rebuked Blake's impatient step in their direction with a chill glance and an even colder tone. 'I'll be with you shortly, Mr Armstrong.'

She didn't know why he was on the ward that morning, but perhaps he wanted to talk to her about Hilda, who was being returned to Cresswell later in the day and should soon start a course of physiotherapy on her stroke-damaged arm and leg. She had been making good progress in the Intensive Care Unit.

'There's no hurry, Sister.' But Blake belied the smooth assurance with a glance at his watch. He didn't mind waiting when someone was genuinely busy. He could recognise a deliberate dawdle when he saw one, he thought dryly.

Keith Oliver had a busy schedule. 'I must be getting along, anyway—I've a conference in ten minutes. I'll arrange to have Mrs Wilcox transferred to the Renal Unit as soon as possible, Sister . . .'

On his way out, he held open the swing door for an approaching nurse. As she entered the ward, Ann's face brightened at sight of Blake, but she knew better than to stop and speak to him under the cold eye of the Ward Sister. Ever since that evening at the Excelsior, she had felt the full force of Jenefer's disapproval and any attempt to talk to her on a personal level had been swept aside with the icy reminder of work waiting to be done. And if that work wasn't done to her satisfaction she came down on her newest junior like a ton of bricks, Ann thought wryly.

Jenefer put out a detaining hand. 'Mrs Moray has a problem with her new walking frame, Nurse. Perhaps you can persuade her to use it as far as the day-room.' That should keep the first-year out of Blake's orbit until he left the ward, she decided. Why should she make it easy for them to conduct their romance on duty when they had every opportunity to meet and talk and make love away from Pagett's?

She continued to keep Blake waiting while she directed another passing nurse towards an elderly patient who was struggling to get out of bed and showing a vast expanse of thigh in the process.

'Go and help Miss Washington, would you, Nurse—and don't forget that she has brittle bones. Be very careful with her,' she warned. Then she turned to Blake, who was regarding her with a hint of satirical amusement in the smile that played about his sensual mouth. 'Now, Mr Armstrong, what can I do for you? As you can see, I'm really very busy . . .'

Blake was disheartened by the impersonal tone, the coolness in her lovely eyes. He couldn't believe what had happened to the warm, lovable, laughing girl he had known in his struggling junior surgeon days at Hartlake. He didn't recognise that girl in the hard, cold, humourless Ward Sister who bitterly refused to be reminded of the days when they had loved each other.

There were moments when he longed to seize her and shake her and sweep her into an embrace that would convince Jenefer once and for all that they belonged together, now and for ever.

This was one of them.

Wryly, he recalled their surroundings and watching patients and hospital etiquette and that she was engaged to someone else—and knew that none of the first considerations would count for anything if the last wasn't an indisputable fact. He would willingly risk his job and everything else to hold her in his arms and know that she still loved him.

The smile that warmed his handsome face betrayed none of those thoughts and feelings. 'I won't take up too much of your time, Sister. Perhaps we could talk in your office . . .?'

Jenefer hesitated. She would feel safer in full view of patients and busy nurses. But she wasn't afraid of being alone with Blake, she told herself firmly—and he wasn't likely to make a pass in the office where they might be interrupted at any moment.

'Yes, of course.' She led the way into the small room, wishing she could trust him not to make a pass at all. But it seemed that the unwilling desire he evoked in her triggered Blake's own fierce sensuality, and he didn't seem to be the kind to respect an engagement ring. His own—or any other man's!

She turned to face him, warily, instinctively putting a hand to the stiff collar of her dark blue dress that concealed the slender gold chain she was wearing about her neck. From it hung the square-cut sapphire in an antique setting that Tom had slipped over her reluctant finger earlier in the week. Only a wedding ring could be worn by a nurse on duty, and she had no wish to flaunt that valuable sapphire, in any case. It seemed a constant reminder to a guilt-ridden Jenefer that she was living a lie.

'I expect you want to talk to me about Mrs Maitland.' Her crisp tone made it clear that she had no intention of discussing anything that wasn't connected with her work.

'Have you heard from ICU? She's well enough to be returned to the ward.' Blake took up the opening gambit because Jenefer always seemed to mellow at the mention of that particular patient, proving that the girl he had once known so well wasn't so very far beneath the surface starch.

'Sister Jennings spoke to me this morning. I've decided to put Mrs Maitland back into the main ward, if you agree. I thought about a side ward, but she's a lady who likes company and she appears to be doing well enough to be with the rest of the patients. You must be very pleased with her progress.' She was talking too much, almost unbending, she realised abruptly. Her fondness for Hilda was her Achilles heel—and Blake was well aware of that fact. It was hard to maintain a chilly reserve in the face of his warm concern for his patient.

'Yes, I am pleased. Her speech is much clearer already and her sight seems to be improving. There's some degree of movement in the damaged arm, too. With good nursing and regular physiotherapy I'm hopeful that she'll make even better progress.' He stood by the panoramic window, contemplating the ward with its bustle of morning rounds. 'She seems annoyed that there isn't more of an improvement, however. I gather she expected an overnight cure,' he added, a trifle dryly.

'Perhaps I overdid the miracle bit,' Jenefer conceded wryly. 'I did warn her that it might be some time before she was mobile or could do much for herself, but I've noticed that patients only hear what they want to hear and shut out the rest.'

'Not only patients, Jenefer.' Blake turned abruptly to look at her through suddenly narrowed eyes. 'Most of us are reluctant to face unpalatable facts. For instance, I find it difficult to accept that you really mean to marry that dry stick.'

She stiffened at the introduction of the personal into discussion of a patient's problems. It was unethical—and unfair! 'Really? I find it easy to believe any number of unpalatable things about you,' she said sweetly.

Blake smiled into the hazel eyes with their intriguing gold flecks and militant sparkle. 'Such as?'

'Never mind,' Jenefer retreated hastily, refusing to be drawn on the subject of his faults and failings. She might find that she loved him still in spite of them . . . She looked away from the lazily smiling depths of dark eyes that seemed to bore right into the heart and soul of her, threatening her resolve to marry Tom and forget the lingering love for an ambitious surgeon. 'The way you live is your business, Blake—and you have to cope with your conscience. I'm just glad it isn't *mine*, that's all!' The impulsive reproach tumbled from her tongue before she could stop herself.

But it had to be said. For she was appalled that he would go to such lengths to get what he wanted out of life—and deeply hurt that his ambitious hopes and dreams still excluded her. Then and now and for always, she thought bleakly.

Blake frowned. 'I don't know what you're talking about.'

'Isn't it obvious? First Cheryl—and now Ann Morley! Nothing stands in the way of what you want, does it?' She couldn't keep the angry bitterness out of her voice.

Anger sparked. 'And what is it that I'm supposed to want so much?'

The sound of the telephone broke across the dangerously silk-soft words. 'Excuse me . . .' Jenefer brushed past him to the desk, feeling threatened by his height and his presence and the disturbing reminders of past intimacy. She lifted the receiver. 'Sister Cresswell speak—oh, Tom! You shouldn't ring me here, you know. I'm very busy . . .'

Hearing the distinct chill of that rebuking tone, Blake wondered if the off-putting manner was just Jenefer slipping automatically into the role of efficient Ward Sister and not the slap-down he had always assumed it to be when he was on the receiving end. For she wouldn't rebuff her fiancé in that way, surely? Or would she?

Blake had his doubts about that engagement. He didn't believe that Jenefer was in love with Cornell or that she would marry him when it came to the crunch. He refused to believe that someone so lovely, so intelligent and sensitive and true, would throw her life away on the wrong man simply because she was too proud and too stubborn to forgive the man who had let her down in the past.

'Tonight? Oh, I see . . . yes, of course, Tom. No, it doesn't matter.' Jenefer kept surprise at the unexpected change of plan from expression and voice. 'I'll ring my mother and let her know. Now, may I talk to you later? I'm up to my eyes! Yes—yes, I will . . . goodbye.' She replaced the receiver, colour in her face. She had been embarrassed, talking to Tom while Blake made not even a polite pretence of not listening.

He stood squarely in the middle of the room, studying her with an enigmatic light in his eyes, tall and powerful and so physical that he stormed her senses. A real man, she thought disloyally, as a familiar ache of longing began in her breast and threatened to consume her entire being.

She had to skirt the surgeon to reach her chair. She needed to put the width of the desk between them, she admitted. 'Now, where were we?'

'*You* were talking to Cornell. Taking him to meet the family?'

Jenefer's chin went up. 'They've met him many times, actually.'

'And they approve?'

'Why shouldn't they?' It was defensive.

Blake sighed. 'My poor darling! Don't they want you to be happy?' he commiserated lightly.

Incensed by the familiar mockery of the most important things in life, Jenefer shot him an indignant glance. 'I suppose you saw at a glance that Tom isn't the right man for me,' she said scathingly.

He smiled. 'I think you can do better for yourself, shall we say?'

'I'm not really interested in what you think, Blake.' She struggled with the thump of a heart that foolishly wanted to read so much more than he meant into the

words. He wasn't promoting *himself*, she told herself
sternly. That was just wishful thinking that made
things so much worse!

'I know you've written me out of your life, but that
doesn't prevent me from wanting you to be happy
with the man you marry, Jenefer.' Unexpectedly,
Blake took her chin between strong fingers and turned
her face so that he could look directly into guarded
hazel eyes. 'I'd like to be sure that you love Cornell.
Do you?'

Taken aback, Jenefer stared at him, her lips framing
an assurance that her heart wouldn't allow her to
utter. She was consumed with a breathless excitement
as she looked into his eyes with their compelling,
heady glow. Heart racing, mouth dry, tingling from
head to toe, she was suddenly weak with longing for
the only man she had ever, could ever, love with all
her heart.

She clutched like a drowning man at the straw of
her pride. 'Of course I'll be happy with Tom. I'm
marrying him for all the right reasons,' she said
stoutly, denying the instinctive protest that pierced
her heart.

It was no answer, but it told Blake all that he needed
to know. Satisfied, he allowed his hand to fall from
her lovely face as his keen ear caught the swish of the
ward door and the soft sound of a step in the corridor.

'I've prescribed a change of drugs for Mrs
Maitland, Sister. Perhaps you would keep a careful
eye on her for a few days in case there are any
unpleasant side-effects from the new cocktail,' he said
easily, the smooth words coinciding with Brenda
Walsh's arrival at the open door.

The staff nurse's knowing glance swept the surgeon
and the slightly flushed Ward Sister. Blake

Armstrong's insistence on having his post-operative patient nursed on a medical ward had caused a wave of speculation among the staff. Brenda didn't subscribe to the general view that it would allow him to see more of Ann Morley. She thought it a pity that Jenefer simply wouldn't be drawn on the fascinating subject of her former friendship with the surgeon.

'Sorry to disturb you, Sister. I know you're busy, but Mrs Maitland is back on the ward and she's asking for you. I'm afraid she's getting agitated.'

'All right, Staff. I'll be there in a few minutes . . .' Hastily, Jenefer donned the mantle of her authority that had been stripped from her during those uncomfortable few minutes with Blake. He made her feel so vulnerable, so helpless, so totally unlike the efficient Ward Sister she had striven so hard to become.

Blake followed her from the office and into the ward. 'We'll continue our conversation in more conducive surroundings and when we both have more time, Sister,' he said lightly.

Protected by the presence of nurses and patients, Jenefer smiled at him. 'Oh, I think we've said all there is to say, Mr Armstrong,' she said sweetly, and swept down the ward to his excited patient.

Hilda waved an agitated greeting as Sister and surgeon neared the bed, face flushed and eyes over-bright, her mouth working in the effort to frame the words that still didn't come easily to mind or tongue.

Jenefer gave her a welcoming hug that ignored etiquette and the prohibiting presence of the senior surgeon. 'It's lovely to have you back with us,' she said warmly. 'And looking so well too! You're a fraud, Hilda.'

'She's certainly doing very well. I'm very pleased

with her progress,' Blake added with smiling approval.

Hilda gurgled and preened herself at the praise, revelling in the attention and admiration of a very attractive man. Jenefer wondered dryly if any woman between the ages of nine and ninety was immune to the charm that had played such havoc with her own life.

The big woman began to thrash about in an attempt to get out of bed and demonstrate the improvement in her mobility in the short time since her operation. It took two nurses to restrain her and her face took on the mulish expression that Jenefer remembered so well. That obstinacy was probably a vital ingredient of the character that refused to be defeated by heart attack or stroke or any other setback, she thought on a rush of affection.

She smiled warmly at the patient whose need for a surgeon's specialist skills had been a link in the chain of destiny that bridged past and present. Whatever happened, there would always be a special place in her thoughts for Hilda.

CHAPTER THIRTEEN

BEAMING, Hilda looked from one to the other of her admiring audience. 'Look . . .' It was strangled but intelligible. Proudly she endeavoured to lift her virtually useless arm by almost an inch, the strain of concentration and determination showing in her flushed face. '*Can* . . . do it,' she muttered fiercely, proving that she could with almost superhuman effort.

She was so proud of such small gain that Jenefer couldn't help being moved. Blinking back tears, she met Blake's tenderly amused gaze. Immediately on the defensive, she overlooked the tenderness and saw only mockery in his dark eyes and recalled how often he had reproached her sentimental involvement with patients in earlier days.

Ward Sisters weren't supposed to show their feelings. So perhaps she wasn't really very good at her job. But at least the patients knew that she had a heart, and surely that mattered more than dignity!

'That's marvellous, Hilda,' she applauded, smiling.

'Carry on like that and you'll soon be able to go home,' added Blake in warm encouragement, but he prescribed a sedative for his over-excited patient.

As a nurse arranged a selection of get-well cards on locker and windowsill at Hilda's forceful direction, Jenefer walked with Blake to the end of the ward.

'I never get used to the miracle of modern medicine,' she said defiantly, still smarting from the amusement of his glance. 'I think it's wonderful what you've managed to do for Hilda!'

'It may not be a lasting improvement,' Blake warned. 'Surgery can temporarily stimulate nerves and reflexes, as I'm sure you know. The miracle happens when good brain cells take over the work of damaged ones, and that can take a very long time. Perhaps too long in Mrs Maitland's case.'

Jenefer was alerted by something in his tone. 'Are you anxious about her?'

'Uneasy, shall we say. I can't put my finger on it, but I'd like you to watch her carefully for a day or two.' His radio-pager bleeped across the words. 'I must get back to the Unit. I'll talk to you later, Sister . . .' In spite of the formal note, his deep voice softened and warmed on the last words, turning them into intimate assurance.

She knew it was foolish, but she went back to Hilda in a daze of delight. For surely there had been a special meaning in his smile and a look of love in those deep-set dark eyes? She walked on air, her heart soaring with a hope that momentarily ignored her engagement to Tom and the existence of Ann Morley.

Grey-faced, somehow shrunk to half her size, Hilda was sunk in pillows, eyes closed and mouth defeated. No doubt she was exhausted by the effort and the excitement of the move from Intensive Care Unit to the familiar ward and the tender loving care of nurses she knew and liked and trusted, Jenefer thought tenderly. But she looked so drawn and so ill to her experienced eye that sudden concern promptly thrust all thought of Blake and an impossible dream from her mind.

She bent over the sick woman. 'Hilda . . .'

Instantly the big woman's eyes opened and she struggled to sit up, anxious to show off her achievement once more. '. . . ook,' she said heavily, her speech slurred and difficult through weariness.

Jenefer laid a gently restraining hand on her shoulder. 'We're all so pleased for you, but you mustn't overdo things, Hilda. It's early days and you really must rest now,' she said firmly. 'You've had a very tiring day.'

Hilda flopped on the pillows with no sign of her usual spirited defiance, obviously having neither energy nor inclination to flout authority. 'Tired . . .' she agreed feebly, closing her eyes, good hand fluttering towards her chest as a slight spasm caught her unawares.

Automatically, Jenefer felt for the pulse with its thready, irregular beat. She saw a familiar look of surprise flicker across Hilda's face and heard the soft sighing release of pent-up breath, and realised with a shock of dismay that the pulse had faltered to a stop beneath her fingers.

Reacting with the instincts of long training, she pressed the panic button to summon help, hurled pillows to the floor and hauled Hilda flat in the bed with a strength born of urgency. She leaned over the collapsed woman, the heel of one hand with the other on top of it pressing down hard on her chest, and began manual respiration, while one nurse ran for the resuscitation trolley and another sped to the telephone and quick-thinking Ann Morley swished curtains about the bed to conceal the emergency from the rest of the ward.

There was no time to rush the patient into a side ward and no time for the tears that threatened Jennifer's dignity. Sentiment was out of place at such a time. All her energy and concentration went into doing what she could for Hilda. Working against the clock, she alternated the rhythmic compression of the chest with the desperate attempt to breathe life into flaccid lungs until she was relieved by the cardiac arrest team. Then she stood back, her own heart pumping wildly, as the doctors went into action with oxygen, cortisone injections and defibrillator.

At some stage in the proceedings, she was aware that Blake was behind her, tense and preoccupied. Jenefer didn't look at him, her attention concentrated on the fight for Hilda's life. Just knowing he was there and as concerned as herself was a help.

After twenty minutes of combined effort, it was silently agreed that nothing more could be done. The cardiac arrest team reluctantly packed up their equipment and went away to await another urgent summons.

Jenefer had desperately willed the silent heart to beat, pumping the vital blood through veins and arteries and encouraging the lungs to work again. She found it hard to accept that such an indomitable spirit had quietly slipped away from the body that had been such a source of frustration and annoyance to a proud woman in the weeks following that debilitating stroke.

She had coped with the death of patients many times in her years of nursing, but Hilda had been special, she grieved, tending the heavy body with loving hands behind drawn curtains while sobered nurses distracted curious or anxious patients with cups of tea and cheerful conversation and routine chores.

As soon as she could, Jenefer retreated to her small sitting-room at the end of the corridor, needing a few minutes to collect herself. She felt Hilda's loss almost as keenly as if she had been a close friend or relative, she admitted, fighting a welling sadness.

Blake entered the room without ceremony a few minutes later, and she turned from the window to look at him through a blur of tears. She seemed so vulnerable, so defenceless, so touchingly young in spite of her Sister's dark blue that he held out his arms to her without a word.

Without hesitation, Jenefer went into them and cried, her face buried against that powerful, reassuring chest, comforted by his closeness and the indistinguishable murmur of unmistakable endearments and the brush of his lips across her hair. Her hard-won Sister's cap, dislodged by that sudden, rushing embrace, lay forgotten and momentarily meaningless on the floor at their feet.

Calmer, she drew away to look up at him through a haze of tears and rueful laughter. 'What shocking behaviour for a Ward Sister! And I haven't cried like that for a patient in years!'

'You're not as hard as you pretend to be, Sister Cresswell.' Blake kissed her then, tenderly, savouring the soft sweetness of her mouth and finding more response than he had dared to dream in the way she relaxed against him and gave him kiss for kiss. His arms tightened about her with a sudden, aching hunger that claimed his woman.

Jenefer clung, arms about his neck, body thrilling to the power and the passion in his embrace, pride and caution thrown to the four winds. Later, she would worry about Tom. Later, she would wonder if Blake cared enough at last to put love before ambition and Ann Morley out of his life. For the moment, all that mattered was his arms about her, his lips on her own, her name murmured with love and longing wrenched from the very depths of the man she had never ceased to love, with all her heart.

At last, reluctantly, she pushed him away. 'Blake, stop! Someone might come in!' she exclaimed on a rush of returning sanity.

'Without knocking,' he drawled, eyes dancing.

'*You* did!'

'So I did—and it paid off, thank God!'

'My defences were down,' Jenefer reproached, but her hazel eyes glowed with delight.

'About time too!' Blake pulled her back into his arms. 'You've been fighting me much too long . . .'

'Oh, Blake!' She was weak with longing as he kissed her, caressed her, stirred her to heady desire as no other man ever had or ever could. It took considerable force of will to ease herself out of arms that felt like home. 'I'm sure we're breaking every rule in the book! What an example to set my nurses!' she exclaimed in breathless self-scolding. She picked up her cap and thrust it on top of thick chestnut curls, fumbling to pin it in place with trembling hands. 'I must get back to the ward. How do I look?' she asked anxiously.

His eyes flattered her with their warm look of love. 'As if you've just been soundly kissed, Sister,' he teased tenderly.

'Oh, dear!' Smiling, Jenefer touched rueful fingers to the burning cheeks, the lips that felt swollen from the tumult of kisses, the pulse that beat quick and hard in the hollow of her throat.

'At least you don't look as if you've been crying on my shoulder,' Blake comforted. 'That *would* shatter your image as the cool-as-cucumber Ward Sister, wouldn't it?'

Reminded of her role and some of the painful duties attached to it, Jenefer instantly sobered. 'Poor Hilda,' she said quietly. 'She wanted so much to get well and go home. She'd just had her first grandchild, you know. It broke her heart that she couldn't hold him in her arms. I felt so sorry for her. I'm sorry for her family too.' She hesitated, choosing her words with care. 'Do you think that surgery made any actual difference to the outcome, Blake?'

'It's hard to say. Even a good heart can be taxed by a long and difficult operation, and she was never an ideal candidate for surgery. You may remember that I had reservations when it was first suggested. Montague was persistent and perhaps I *was* guilty of operating just to prove a point, as you said. But I had the patient's best interests at heart, of course—and I believed she stood a reasonable chance of a good recovery.'

'It isn't anyone's fault that her heart failed so suddenly,' Jenefer pointed out in swift, loving loyalty.

'No. Hearts are unpredictable organs,' Blake agreed wryly.

Impulsively she stood on tiptoe to kiss the tall surgeon who was so dear, so loved. 'That's why I gave mine away years ago,' she said softly, discarding pride, the golden glow of her smile lighting up her lovely face.

For the rest of the day Jenefer was haunted by that slight smile of satisfaction in the dark eyes that had watched her hurry down the corridor to the ward. She had gone into Blake's arms, kissed him back, virtually thrown herself at him in an abandon of loving that nullified her claim to be happily engaged to Tom—and she still had no idea how Blake really felt about her in return, she agonised.

Blake was her man, the love of her life, the only man who could truly make her happy, she knew. But their ways might still lead in different directions. He hadn't changed. He wanted prestige, power, wealth—and Jenefer feared that they were still more important to him than she could ever be. He had married Cheryl for the promise of those things. Now it seemed that he was courting Ann Morley for the same reason.

So where did *she* stand? How could she trust the look in his eyes, the longing in his touch, the implication of a love that he would probably deny for the sake of ambition all over again?

She was thankful to go off duty at the end of the day. She whisked through Main Hall, smiling absent response to a porter's goodnight, and passed through opening doors into the scented air of a beautiful spring evening. Flowering cherry scattered its delicate drift of blossom over her head and shoulders as she walked towards the car park.

She had almost reached her Fiat before she saw Blake, leaning against its brown bonnet, hands in his pockets and a lazy smile in his dark eyes as he waited for her to reach him.

He straightened, his smile deepening and reaching out in warm welcome. 'Hallo, Jenny.'

No one else had ever called her that. He said the small name with a tenderness that warmed and disarmed her and dispelled the terrible anxiety that had heavied her heart. She felt as if he had put both arms about her and led her home.

A swift, golden smile that brimmed with love illumined her grave face. 'Hallo, Blake.'

The simple exchange was regret and forgiving and a new beginning all in one.

Blake put an arm about her with the casual intimacy of a lover. 'Come and have a drink.'

Jenefer didn't protest as he led her towards the Winchester Arms. She had no reason to hurry home to an empty flat and a long, dull evening. Besides, it felt so right to be walking at Blake's side, his arm draped in careless affection about her shoulders just as in those earlier days when the merging of their lives had seemed the destiny they had been born to fulfil.

She smiled up at him as they waited at the kerb for a break in the steady stream of traffic. Blake's arm tightened about her and then he shifted his hand from her shoulder to curve about her bright head in brief, tender caress, his long fingers stroking her soft cheek. The look in his eyes gladdened Jenefer's loving heart.

She studied him as he stood at the bar, turning occasionally to smile or to raise a tolerant eyebrow at the slowness of the service. It was the busy hour for the pub staff, packed with off-duty doctors and nurses as well as friends and relatives of Pagett's patients whiling away the last half-hour to visiting time.

Blake stood out in the crowd, not only because of his height and those broad shoulders and the striking good looks. Jenefer felt she could pick him out in a football stadium filled with thousands, guided by the instinct of heart and blood and the senses that quickened at the mere thought of him.

Blake brought the drinks, his lager and her Martini, and set them on the table. Then he slid on to the cushioned seat at her side. Relaxed, content, he smiled at her warmly.

'*Don't* say it's just like old times,' Jenefer forestalled lightly, indulgent affection in her hazel eyes.

He raised his glass. 'I was about to say—here's to the future. Whatever it holds for us.'

It was too vague for her liking. She would gladly drink to a future that he promised they should share. But those evasive words filled her with a familiar doubt and foreboding. She knew that he wanted her—but how much and for how long?

'Life plays some strange tricks,' she said slowly. 'Who would have thought that we'd be having a friendly drink together, six years later?'

'If it was sixty years, I'd still feel the same way about you,' Blake said quietly. He reached for her hand and enfolded it within strong fingers. 'You're special, Jenny. You always were and you always will be.'

But how special? Jenefer wondered heavily. Could she compete with the ambition that had apparently already chosen another wife? Withdrawing her hand, she picked up her drink. 'Tom has been telling me about Max Morley's plans for a clinic,' she said with a deliberate change of subject that mentioned Tom and let Blake know that she was aware of his hopes in one direction, at least.

Blake nodded. 'Interesting idea, don't you think? Max has been trying to talk me into becoming a director, but I'm not ready to commit myself. The place isn't yet built and may never be anything more than pie in the sky, after all.'

'I'm not sure that I approve of private hospitals that cream off the best doctors and nurses from the Health Service,' Jenefer said doubtfully.

'It's a valid point of view. But having worked bloody awful hours for little except job satisfaction for too many years, most surgeons expect to combine public and private work by the time they reach my stage in their careers,' said Blake, smiling.

'You've known the Morleys for some time, I suppose?' It was carefully casual, but she desperately needed to know the real extent of his relationship with Ann Morley, in particular.

'Well, I've known Ann for years, of course. She

used to share a flat with Cheryl. Ann didn't have much to do with her family in those days. Max wanted to treat her like a princess and she wanted to earn her own bread.'

'I admire her for that, anyway.'

Blake nodded. 'Oh, she's a very independent girl. She and Max get on better now that she's nursing. He approves of that as a career for his daughter.'

'She'll make a very good nurse,' Jenefer assured him generously.

'I'm sure she will.' Blake smiled. 'She reminds me very much of a certain first-year at Hartlake in my junior surgeon days. She'll be treading on your heels in a few years, Sister Cresswell!'

'I don't doubt it.' Her smile was slightly forced. She loved her job, but it played very little part in the dreams of a life spent with Blake that he had rekindled with his kisses. It was disconcerting to realise that he thought her wedded to a nursing career! 'You're very good friends, aren't you?'

'Yes, we are. I don't know what I'd have done without Ann at times,' Blake said frankly. 'I admire her tremendously. She stands by her principles. Do you know, she won't accept even the smallest allowance from Max, for all his millions?'

'But she's living at home, isn't she?'

'For the time being—and mainly for my benefit, in fact. The Manor is a convenient roof over both our heads until we find something more suitable. At the moment I'm negotiating for a house near the golf course,' he explained.

Jenefer felt the implication of the words like a physical blow. Although she had already suspected his intentions, the confirmation was the total destruction of those newly-revived and very foolish dreams. She was much too proud to let him see her hurt, however.

'House-hunting is always a problem, isn't it?' she agreed brightly. 'Fortunately it won't arise for Tom and me. He already has a beautiful house just outside town—Stonewalls.'

Blake's eyes widened abruptly. He had been so impatient for the evening when they would be together and he could tell her how much he loved and needed her, how anxious he was to marry her, how impossible it was for her to marry another man when she had belonged to him in every way that mattered since her nineteenth birthday. They were born to be lovers; destiny had given them a second chance of happiness, and he couldn't believe what he was hearing as Jenefer talked so blithely about the house she would share with Cornell, once they were married.

Why had she gone into his arms, returned kiss for kiss, virtually admitted that she had always loved him, if it meant nothing? She did love him! Damn it, he knew it in his bones!

But it seemed that she had no faith in his power to be a good husband, to make her happy and keep her secure—and how could he blame her? She had trusted him once and he had let her down. She had given him heart and soul and beautiful body, and he had walked out of her life as if he had never valued that precious gift. Was it so surprising that Jenefer had made up her mind to marry Cornell and nothing he could say or do would sway her from that resolve?

'Stonewalls, did you say?' He drained his lager and set down the glass with a slam. 'It sounds the perfect place to imprison a bride,' he said brutally.

Jenefer flinched and then laughed. 'How dramatic, Blake! And unlikely! Tom isn't the kind to lock me away in an ivory tower—or to lay down rules and insist that I obey them. He's kind and generous and reliable and . . .'

'A paragon, obviously,' Blake interrupted mockingly. 'But I doubt if he'd approve if he saw you drinking with a former lover. Few men are that generous.' He got to his feet. 'So I'll say goodnight and good luck, Sister—before the place begins to buzz with the kind of talk that's bound to reach your fiancé's ears!'

The pub door swung to and fro behind him and Jenefer sat very still, swallowing shock but with anger ripping through her at the way Blake had walked out on her.

Just like before.

Just as he always would.

CHAPTER FOURTEEN

JENEFER was roused from a muddled dream of Blake and Hilda and Brenda Walsh by the persistent ringing of the telephone beside her bed. Reluctantly she emerged from the covers and stretched out a hand to silence it.

'Sister Cresswell . . .' she mumbled sleepily.

'Jenefer! Thank God!'

'Go away, Blake. I don't want to talk to you,' she said crossly, and put down the receiver, too sleepy to wonder at the relief in his deep voice. She turned over, irritated. Whatever he wanted, it was much too late. Or too early. He had no right to ring her up in the middle of the night, in any case. Even to apologise.

The telephone rang again as Jenefer punched the pillow she had been hugging in mistake for the surgeon who insisted on invading her dreams.

'What *do* you want?' she snapped, snatching it up. 'I do wish you'd leave me alone!'

'Don't ring off, Jenefer. I've a good reason for calling.'

The urgency in his tone alerted her instantly. 'What . . .? What is it?'

'I'm afraid it's bad news, Jenny,' he said gently.

She sat up, colour draining from her face. 'Go on.'

'I've just had a call from Casualty. It's Cornell . . . he crashed his car and injured his head, and I'm needed to operate right away.' Blake didn't mean to sound so blunt, so unfeeling. There was no easy way to break the news.

Jenefer felt as though she had been kicked in the chest by a horse. All the breath was shocked out of her by Blake's bald announcement and she found it impossible to speak.

'Jenny . . .?'

She took a deep, hurting breath and managed to find her voice. 'Is he bad? Is he seriously ill?' Euphemism for near to death, she thought heavily, steeling herself.

'Bad enough. I wasn't sure if you knew—if anyone had been in touch. Damn it, I didn't even know that you were home! Apparently there was a woman with him . . .' Blake broke off, fighting a flood of emotion.

'I'll be there as soon as I can be.' Jenefer swung her feet to the floor on the words.

'Darling, is that wise? I know you're anxious, but . . .'

'Blake, I'm engaged to him!' It wasn't the right time to melt inside at the tender warmth of that caressing endearment. Sternly, she pinned her thoughts to Tom, lying on a hospital trolley and waiting to be taken into Theatres or perhaps already prepped and anaesthetised in readiness for Blake's arrival.

'No need to remind me,' Blake said quietly, his tone wry. 'Of course you want to be on hand. I'll pick you up on my way—I don't want you driving. Ten minutes?'

'I'll be ready.' Hearing the click of the replaced receiver at his end, Jenefer swung into action. At times like these, her training was invaluable.

Without even thinking about it, she had put on her dark blue uniform dress and dragged a brush hastily through her tousled curls and thrust her feet into hospital brogues, then stood waiting outside the door as the car drew up at the house.

It was half past two in the morning. The streets were empty and silent and Blake drove fast but carefully, hands steady on the steering wheel and eyes intent on the ribbon of road that led to Pagett's.

Jenefer wanted to hold on to him, but she kept her hands tightly locked in her lap. She wanted to talk to him, but the only words that came to her lips were of love and need and longing, and they were so dreadfully out of place when Tom was ill and injured and possibly dying at that very moment.

She didn't realise that she was wearing her engagement ring until it began to wink in the light from street lamps that fell at regular intervals across her folded hands. She didn't need to be reminded that she was engaged to Tom, she thought bleakly, wondering if some prick of conscience or some vague sense of rightness had prompted her to take the sparkling sapphire ring from the chain that lay on her dressing-table and slip it on her finger in unconscious action.

'All right . . .?' Blake turned his head to smile, to reassure and comfort. He was concerned about her stillness, her silence. She was shocked, of course. She was worried about Cornell, naturally.

Even if she didn't really love the man.

She was possibly guilt-ridden as well as anxious, he thought with tender perception. She wore Cornell's ring, but Blake knew in his blood and in his bones that Jenefer had never ceased to love him all these years, and he cursed the quick temper that had flared at her proud insistence on marrying another man in spite of her destiny.

He had handled her badly since the first moment of meeting again, caring so much that he was clumsy with her fragile pride, saying and doing all the wrong things and driving her into another man's arms. How could she be expected to understand or to believe that he loved her more than life itself?

The Casualty Officer who had called from Pagett's had spoken of a woman in Cornell's crashed car, but had rung off without offering any clues to her identity. Blake had immediately wondered if Jenefer had fled to her fiancé for consolation after he had left her so cavalierly in the pub. He never again wanted to experience anything like those agonising moments of waiting for Jenefer's telephone to be lifted and Jenefer's voice to assure him that she was safe and sound.

'I'm frightened, Blake.' Jenefer said it low, shakily. She was desperately trying not to think, not to dwell on the horror that Tom might die or might never be the same man again after an injury to his head. But she couldn't stop *feeling* . . .

Instantly Blake's hand reached out to clasp her trembling fingers and she drew strength from his touch, his presence, his silent assurance that he was and always would be *there* when needed.

He brought the soft-purring Mercedes to a halt outside the entrance to Accident and Emergency. Jenefer turned her face into his strong shoulder for a moment, comforted by the scent of tweed, the maleness of him. Blake ran a hand lightly over her soft hair, paused to cradle her cheek in a caress, patted her shoulder.

'You know that I'll do what I can . . .' He left the rest unsaid. They both knew that a surgeon could only do his best. Miracles were beyond him, no matter how much faith a patient or nurse might have in his ability.

'I know.' Jenefer caught at his hand, held it briefly to her cheek. It was an admission of love and a gesture of farewell. Straightening, she took firm hold of herself as she relinquished a dream for the reality of a promise made to a man who might need her more than ever in the future.

Accident and Emergency never slept. Even at that hour, a young couple huddled anxiously over a wailing baby and a man with a blood-soaked handkerchief held to a cut above his eye waited to be seen by the Casualty Officer on duty.

Blake spoke to the agency staff nurse behind the big reception desk. At the sound of his voice Mike Lloyd, doctor on duty just like the last occasion when they had rushed a casualty to Pagett's for attention, came out of a cubicle. The billowing curtains revealed an elderly woman in nightdress and curlers who lay shocked and grey-faced under blankets on the couch.

'You moved fast,' Mike approved. 'But I'm afraid your patient's already in Theatres. His condition suddenly worsened and he's having surgery for a punctured lung while the NSU team stand by until you get there.'

'Tell them I'm on my way.' As Jenefer began to follow him towards the connecting lift, Blake checked and turned to her with a warning light in his dark eyes. 'I'm sorry, sweetheart, I don't want you in the theatre,' he said gently but sternly.

She didn't argue. She had never felt less inclined to venture into an operating theatre or less equipped to assist, if he had asked it of her, she thought ruefully. She hated to admit it, but the capable Sister Cresswell had gone completely to pieces!

'You'll let me know what's happening?' she asked anxiously, feeling sick and shaky and very, very cold.

'Of course I will!' Blake found and held her hand for a brief, reassuring moment. Then he stepped into the waiting lift.

Jenefer wandered back to the desk, already missing his supportive presence, wondering how she would get through the hours until she knew if Tom was going to be all right.

Mike completed a request for X-rays for the elderly woman patient and then handed the form to the staff nurse. Turning to Jenefer, he cast a professional eye over her tense figure and pale face. 'Feeling OK, Sister?'

'Yes . . . yes, I'm fine.' She managed a smile. 'It's just—there's nothing I can do but wait, apparently. The hardest part of all.'

'I daresay we can find something for you to do to pass the time, eh, Staff?' Mike winked at the nurse behind the desk. 'Never a dull moment in A & E! For instance, you could try persuading Mrs Lomax to let us keep her in overnight for observation. She's being very difficult.'

Jenefer frowned. 'Mrs Lomax . . .?'

The nurse jerked her head in the direction of a cubicle with drawn curtains. 'The MP's wife. She's in there with a broken wrist. She was in the car with Mr Cornell—I expect that's why she won't let us call her husband,' she added with a sardonic smile.

As an agency nurse, she was unaware that the injured man was Sister Gale's fiancé. She did wonder why the CO suddenly frowned at her, however.

'I'll have a word . . .' Jenefer didn't know what she was expected to say to someone she only knew by sight, but it would give her something else to do than think and worry about Tom.

She went towards the cubicle, puzzled by the staff

nurse's nudging words. The implication was obvious but, knowing Tom, she doubted that there was anything underhand in his association with the MP's wife. Yet it *was* curious that she didn't want her husband told that she'd been involved in an accident while travelling in Tom's car.

She drew back the curtains. 'Mrs Lomax?'

Nicola Lomax had a rapidly blackening bruise on her beautiful cheek and a smudge of dried blood across her mouth. A cloud of dark hair fell wildly about her face and shoulders. Her red dress was torn and muddy and bloody and she crouched in a chair, nursing her painful wrist while she waited for the results of X-rays and news of Tom.

She looked up quickly as Jenefer entered the cubicle. 'I thought you were the nurse . . .' Her face darkened.

'I'm Sister Gale. How are you feeling, Mrs Lomax?' Jenefer didn't know why she fell back on the briskly efficient role of Ward Sister, unless it was those accusing eyes and the sullen hostility in the woman's attitude.

'I know who you are,' Nicola said rudely. 'I've seen you with Tom enough times. How is he, anyway?'

'He's in the operating theatre at the moment. I don't know any more than that, Mrs Lomax. As soon as there's any news . . .'

'I don't suppose you'll tell me!' It was a bitter, angry retort.

'You must be very concerned about him,' Jenefer said gently, seeing shock in the dark eyes and the wild tone, more than pain from her injured wrist in the distraught way she rocked herself back and forth in the chair. 'I'm sure he'll be all right. He's in very good hands.' Her tone was kind, soothing. She didn't understand the woman's distress, but it was a nurse's job to calm and comfort in every situation.

'I don't want him to—to *die*!' Nicola said on a low, sobbing moan.

'I don't think there's any risk of that,' Jenefer reassured her, although she was far from confident that Tom could survive surgery to remove a piece of shattered bone that was pressing on a vital part of the brain, in spite of Blake's skill and expertise.

Nicola abruptly reared her head. 'I suppose you think he'll marry you!' She threw the jealous words at the serene hospital Sister who seemed so cool, so untroubled, while Tom lay at death's door in an operating theatre. 'Well, he *won't*! I'll see to that!'

Jenefer slim fingers went involuntarily to the heavy ring on her left hand, turned it round and round. 'That's something to be talked about when Tom is better, don't you think?' she suggested quietly. But her heart jumped at the possibility that Tom loved this woman more than herself. It would explain so much—his coldness, his contentment with a platonic relationship all these months, his sensed reluctance to marry her in the face of her insistence that it was what they both wanted.

'Do you think he loves you? Silly girl!' Nicola's laugh was cruel. 'He's been using you to throw dust in my husband's eyes! Giles is so jealous that I mustn't even look at another man! Well, I've done more than look at Tom. We're lovers—and have been for months! How do you feel about *that*, Sister?' She tossed the hair from her face, her eyes hard as she challenged Jenefer with the mocking words.

Jenefer felt very grateful that she wasn't in love with Tom. It might have been unbearable hurt to learn of his affair with another woman in such a way. As it was, she could end their engagement without the slightest pang of heart or conscience—as soon as Tom recovered. What he did then was entirely up to him—and Giles Lomax.

But what an eye-opener! Tom of all men to be carrying on a sordid affair with another man's wife while looking as if butter wouldn't melt in his mouth—and she had thought him so straight, so reliable, so trustworthy!

Had he really been using her, as Nicola Lomax claimed? Well, if that was the case, she couldn't be angry about it, because she had used Tom too. To protect her vulnerable emotions from attack by other men and, since Blake's advent, to keep her pride from crumbling before the onslaught of renewed love and need.

'I expect you'd like some tea,' she said kindly, putting her hand on the woman's shoulder. The shock of the accident combined with dread for her lover had left her unnerved and overwrought. Tea and sympathy were still excellent medicine in such cases, in Jenefer's view. 'I'll see if I can arrange it.'

She closed the curtains behind her, smiling at the staff nurse who had probably strained every nerve to listen. In spite of her fears for Tom, she felt as if a huge weight had suddenly slipped from her shoulders. She didn't know what the future held for her, but it must be better than marriage to a man she didn't love!

She didn't seem to have much luck with engagements, she thought wryly, as she slipped the sapphire ring from her finger and into her dress pocket.

Third time lucky, perhaps.

Nicola Lomax jumped up and put her head through the gap in the chintz curtains. 'Tell them to ring my husband!' she called after the departing Sister. 'I'm not staying here and it doesn't matter if he *does* know, does it? He'll have read my letter by now, anyway!' As Jenefer turned to look at her, her chin tilted. 'We were going away together! We love each other!'

The defiant words rang out across the big room with its benches and curtained cubicles and busy staff. The Casualty Officer and the staff nurse exchanged glances. The girl with the baby stopped her rocking and murmuring for a startled moment. The shabby tramp making his way to the desk on the arm of a solicitous policeman forgot to limp. A nurse giggled. A porter glanced back and clipped the door with the trolley that held the elderly woman he was taking to the X-ray Department. The man with the bloodstained pad held to his eyebrow got unsteadily to his feet.

'Hey, Doc! Do you want me to bleed to death?' he demanded aggressively. 'I've been sat here a good hour while you chat up the bleeding nurses!'

With a sigh, Mike indicated an empty cubicle. 'In here . . .' he said peremptorily. He caught the eye of a passing nurse. 'Nurse! Would you clean up this man's face, please. I'll be back in a moment.'

Jenefer leaned on the reception desk to speak to the staff nurse. 'How serious is the injury to Mrs Lomax's wrist? Do we know yet?'

The girl picked up a folder. 'We've just had the results of the X-rays. It's a simple Colles fracture, Sister. Someone's coming down to put on a plaster. Then she can go home if that's what she wants.'

'Then she won't need an anaesthetic?'

'Only a local.'

'Good. I promised her a cup of tea. Could you spare a nurse to make it, Staff? Thanks very much.' She turned to Mike. 'Do you have her home number? It might be as well to let her husband know she's here and what's happened. If he doesn't come to collect her, I expect you can find her a bed for the night, can't you?' Her smile was coaxing.

He executed a mock salute. 'Here to serve, Sister. All things to all men—*and* women,' he assured her dryly.

'Would you like some tea, Sister?' The staff nurse had been filled in on the facts by Mike Lloyd during the few minutes that Jenefer had spent with the woman in the cubicle. She was agog to hear more at first hand.

Jenefer shook her head. 'No, I don't think so, thanks. I'm going to see how they're getting on in Theatres. I know it's too soon for any news, but at least I'll be on the spot.'

Wearing greens and theatre cap, she peered through the small round window in the operating-room door. Both teams of surgeons were busy with their separate procedures. Tom was just a shape on the table, covered by green drapes. Jenefer watched the steady movements of skilled hands, the turn of capped heads as surgeons consulted, the border activity of busy theatre nurses.

Blake was easily identified with those broad shoulders straining the seams of his gown, tendrils of black hair escaping from his cap to dance on the nape of his neck. Opening the door a fraction, Jenefer heard the hiss and purr of the respirator and the steady bleep of a monitor, the low murmur of voices and the familiar chink of instruments tossed into a receiver after use.

She stole into the room to stand at the back of the theatre, so still and quiet that she was unnoticed by

the intent surgeons. She was approached by a theatre
nurse who went away as soon as Jenefer explained her
identity. A murmur rippled round the room, glances
followed and nods of acceptance from the theatre
team. Blake looked over his shoulder at her and she
saw a frown leap to his dark eyes. He'd asked her to
keep away and she'd agreed. But he would understand
her need to be present after all, she felt. She didn't
want to be a distraction, but perhaps her love and her
faith in him could help to further a brilliant surgeon's
career.

She sent up a silent prayer.

For Tom.

For those clever, caring hands to achieve yet
another miracle of surgery.

For future happiness for herself and the man she
loved with all her heart . . .

One set of surgeons finished removing the broken
rib that had pierced Tom's lung and left the theatre
long before the delicate craniotomy procedure neared
its end. Through the quiet hours of the night and into
the early morning, a dedicated surgeon drew on all his
knowledge and skill and concentration to save the life
of the man he still regarded as a rival.

The sun was steadily climbing towards the roof of
the Pagett Foundation Hospital when his patient was
finally wheeled from the theatre to the Intensive Care
Unit to begin the process of recovery. Blake walked
into the annexe, drawing the green gown from his
broad shoulders and dropping it into the dirty bin.
Damp patches darkened his green tunic with its
V-neck and short sleeves. Muscular bare arms
glistened with sweat and his black curls clung damply
to his brow and his neck.

Tired but euphoric with the conviction that the

long operation had been a success, he smiled at the girl who followed him into the annexe, slender figure concealed beneath the thin theatre dress, lovely hair bundled into a mob cap, grave face pale with weariness and tension.

Blake had never ceased to be aware of her vigil at the back of the theatre, supporting him with her touching faith in his ability. As always, he had risen to the challenge. For his patient. For the sake of his reputation as a star surgeon. For the woman he loved.

'He'll do,' he said simply.

Jenefer regarded him steadily, her eyes bright with love and trust and gratitude. 'Thank you, Blake.'

He stretched out a hand to touch her cheek in tender caress. 'I didn't save him so you could marry him,' he warned, smiling. 'He's not getting *my* girl!'

A smile dawned in the hazel eyes with their intriguing gold glints. 'No. That was a mistake,' she agreed.

'We've made too many mistakes—both of us. Things will be different in the future,' Blake told her firmly. He drew her towards him.

Jenefer lifted her face for the surgeon's kiss, the seal on their love, the promise for the future, the commitment to each other that nothing and nobody would ever break again.

Doctor Nurse Romances

Romance in modern medical life

Read more about the lives and loves of doctors and nurses in the fascinatingly different backgrounds of contemporary medicine. These are the three Doctor Nurse romances to look out for next month.

VET IN CHARGE
Mary Bowring

BAPTISM OF FIRE
Stella Whitelaw

TROPICAL DOCTOR
Margaret Barker

Buy them from your usual paperback stockist, or write to: Mills & Boon Reader Service, P.O. Box 236, Thornton Rd, Croydon, Surrey CR9 3RU, England. Readers in Southern Africa — write to: Independent Book Services Pty, Postbag X3010, Randburg, 2125, S. Africa.

Mills & Boon
the rose of romance

AROUND THE WORLD WORDSEARCH
COMPETITION!

How would you like a years supply of Mills & Boon Romances ABSOLUTELY FREE? Well, you can win them! All you have to do is complete the word puzzle below and send it in to us by October 31st. 1989. The first 5 correct entries picked out of the bag after that date will win **a years supply of Mills & Boon Romances** (*ten books every month - worth around £150*) What could be easier?

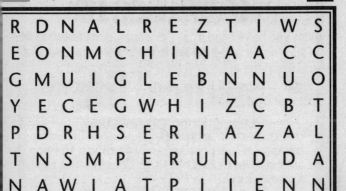

R	D	N	A	L	R	E	Z	T	I	W	S
E	O	N	M	C	H	I	N	A	A	C	C
G	M	U	I	G	L	E	B	N	N	U	O
Y	E	C	E	G	W	H	I	Z	C	B	T
P	D	R	H	S	E	R	I	A	Z	A	L
T	N	S	M	P	E	R	U	N	D	D	A
N	A	W	I	A	T	P	I	I	E	N	N
Y	L	A	T	I	N	A	N	A	N	A	D
N	G	S	T	N	H	Y	D	E	M	L	Q
W	N	O	J	A	M	A	I	C	A	L	A
R	E	L	A	D	A	N	A	C	R	O	R
T	H	A	I	L	A	N	D	D	K	H	I

ITALY	THAILAND	SCOTLAND	SWITZERLAND
GERMANY	IRAQ	JAMAICA	
HOLLAND	ZAIRE	TANZANIA	**PLEASE TURN**
BELGIUM	TAIWAN	PERU	**OVER FOR**
EGYPT	CANADA	SPAIN	**DETAILS**
CHINA	INDIA	DENMARK	**ON HOW**
NIGERIA	ENGLAND	CUBA	**TO ENTER**

HOW TO ENTER

All the words listed overleaf, below the word puzzle, are hidden in the grid. You can find them by reading the letters forward, backwards, up or down, or diagonally. When you find a word, circle it or put a line through it, the remaining letters (which you can read from left to right, from the top of the puzzle through to the bottom) will spell a secret message.

After you have filled in all the words, don't forget to fill in your name and address in the space provided and pop this page in an envelope (you don't need a stamp) and post it today. Hurry - competition ends October 31st. 1989.

Mills & Boon Competition,
FREEPOST,
P.O. Box 236,
Croydon,
Surrey. CR9 9EL
Only one entry per household

Secret Message _____

_____

Name _____

Address _____

_____

_____

_____ Postcode _____

You may be mailed as a result of entering this competition

COMP 6